HUNTER IN HUSKVARNA

SARA STRIDSBERG

HUNTER IN HUSKVARNA

Translated from the Swedish by
Deborah Bragan-Turner

MACLEHOSE PRESS
QUERCUS · LONDON

First published in the Swedish language as *Hunter I Huskvarna* by Albert Bonniers
Forlag, Stockholm, in 2021
First published in Great Britain in 2024 by

MacLehose Press
an imprint of Quercus
Carmelite House
50 Victoria Embankment
London EC4Y 0DZ

The cost of this translation was supported by a subsidy
from the Swedish Arts Council, gratefully acknowledged.

SWEDISH
ARTSCOUNCIL

A CIP catalogue record for this book is available from the British Library.

ISBN (PB) 978 1 52942 326 6
ISBN (eBook) 978 1 52942 327 3

10 9 8 7 6 5 4 3 2 1

Designed and typeset in Minion by Libanus Press Ltd
Printed and bound in Great Britain by Clays Ltd, Elcograf S.p.A.

MIX
Paper from
responsible sources
FSC® C104740

Papers used by MacLehose Press are from well-managed forests and other
responsible sources.

Contents

HUNTER IN HUSKVARNA

There were huge, dark mountains that dominated the town, casting a special kind of darkness as they stretched steeply up into the sky. There was also God. And there was the firearms factory, which swallowed men up in the morning and spat them out again in the afternoon, when the siren sounded and a flood of people poured out of the building's jaws and then dispersed. After a while the town would soak them up and they would become part of the mass of people wandering around, but for the time being they were just something the factory spewed out when it had finished with them.

I used to stand and watch them coming out of the factory. They wound their way forward as one single man, like smoke, like something flowing, a tide. And then I walked back to the waterfalls, where we lived in those days. Immediately before the falls was the black river, cold and sleek and filled with tiny leopard-spotted leeches that would latch onto our legs, with an electric current in its shallow, muddy water. I would linger at the river, because under the trees there was a special feeling that you couldn't find anywhere else, the deep dark of lions, velvet shadows, a snake lying in the sun, glinting, empty beer cans someone had shot at. The marks left by the bullets showed on the tree trunks, black wounds in the birch trees' delicate skin. It was the factory that made this region inviting, that drew people to move in from the forests all around. And God, naturally, he still retained his appeal here. There were places he was less popular, in Stockholm, for example, where we had lived before, where he had been superseded by pop stars, and stock market crashes, and romantic love, but here he was still someone. In the mornings we prayed on our school benches, and then Miss Elly stomped the day into action on the organ; and it groaned and squealed, and she looked as though she was battling with a giant angel. I don't know if anyone believed in those prayers and hymns, but they could scarcely have done any harm. The only one who didn't pray was Hunter: his hands lay open on the desk and he looked out of the window, his gaze following the birds rising from the enormous ash tree. When I glanced over at him by the window, he was immersed in himself; he could already do that, disappear into himself, as if in a dream. At that moment you wanted to be there with him.

My parents were called The Atheists, though they didn't know it themselves, and it sounded a bit like we were a pop group. Hunter's father always sat in the square outside the Rosen Hotel, and he shouted to us when we went past, and so we always sat down and listened to him and his colleagues, that was what he called them, and they would give us a few coins and we would run errands for them, buy shirt studs and snus and fetch hamburgers. We would sit there for a while on our way home from school, and Hunter was always so calm, sitting there on the very edge of the bench, with a patience and attentiveness he never showed with me. I knew he was just waiting to go, but he would never say so, never snub his father and his father's friends. I wouldn't either, I admired those men who were a little apart from the world, who had renounced everything and had done so with pride. They used to laugh at the people still working in the factory, the way they toadied to the higher-ups who had the power, and I think it ingrained in me the belief in that sort of life as an ideal, an intrinsic direction to follow, even if I would later take a different course myself. Hunter's father had worked in the factory in the beginning. Like everyone else, I was going to say, but that's how it was, the factory was the heart of the town. Then one day he just stopped going, and instead he went down to the centre of town in his work overalls. Sooner or later a person couldn't face what lay in store for them, so turned off onto another road and continued on that path. My parents were pen-pushers, as I too would eventually become. I scuttled along in their footsteps like a little rat, without looking back. Hunter's mother had left in the early days and was never heard of again. Some said she was in Ryhov Hospital, or the churchyard, but Hunter said that she'd just become fed up, and he understood. Had his father not needed him, he too would have left on the E4 motorway and headed south in a truck, he said. In the meantime he was rescuing dogs. He took them from the centre of town and released them in the forest. With me Hunter was often somewhere else, buried inside himself, as if the world really had nothing to do with him, and he didn't always answer when I said something. I thought it was because he liked me best out of everyone. But then he could suddenly be so close it scared me, when we were sitting above the thundering falls at night and he looked at me with his big dark eyes.

"Why are you with me?"

I have never forgotten the twilight conversations on the benches. No-one had ever spoken to me the way they did there. It was never anything special, but somehow Hunter's father could always weave what we said into something else, and all at once we were in a bigger story and my voice was one with other voices.

"You sound like Selma Lagerlöf," he used to say to me. "What a classy little friend you've got, Hunter. Hold on to her and everything'll be just fine. Little Selma Lagerlöf."

We would sit with Hunter's father for a few hours, before wandering on into what was our life. It didn't add up to much: the invariable circuits of the town centre, the roar of the falls where we would stand with our bicycles, the porn magazines we stashed in the forest. There were times when we arrived and somebody had got there before us. Then you would wait, or you would rush forward shouting at the top of your voice, and the little boy or girl would run away, their knickers around their ankles. Sometimes it was an adult, and we would wait behind the trees until they had finished. Then we would go up and sniff at the old magazines, their pages exuding a stale but quite exquisite smell. Hunter and I did everything together, even this. While we read and pleasured ourselves, we didn't know that was what we were doing; this took place before we knew about sex. Everything was a game, nothing was real, not for Hunter either, I don't think. We had just discovered the sweetness we could evoke in one another. Sometimes more people turned up, shadows, hiding behind the white trunks of the birch trees. And hovering over the whole thing was God, watching us as we lay beneath the towering beech trees, and I don't know what he thought, though I shouldn't imagine he was particularly interested. But people here were obsessed with him. On every corner there was a little church with a blue neon cross. Everybody believed in the same God in those days. When children squinted upwards they could see angels gliding through the air. I never saw any, but I didn't tell the others that. And in a way God was rather like those magazines full of bosoms: a pretext for being together.

Hunter picked up dogs that were tethered outside buildings in the centre and took them out of town, where he let them go; I went with him sometimes. When we were heading back to town, the dog would watch us like an alien being in the wide landscape, surprised and uncertain about what it should do with the freedom. I don't really remember my parents during this phase with Hunter and the dogs. My life unfolded apart from them, but it was as though they expanded in their absence, they became both more unfamiliar and more definite, as if our childhood waxed as we grew up. I always thought I would leave too one day. I couldn't see myself living forever between these mountains. But I stayed nonetheless.

When darkness fell we were on the motorway slip road in black binbags, waiting to see if the cars would run us over.

"Are you scared?" I asked, inside my sack.

"No. Are you?"

"A bit, maybe. Not very. Do you think it'll be quick?"

"Really quick. Like heaven."

"Do you believe in heaven?"

He was silent inside his sack.

"What if it only gets one of us?"

I heard him breathing next to me inside the plastic, but when a car approached we always ended up leaping for our lives into the ditch, where we crouched until we heard the car pass. We didn't want to die, we just wanted something to happen, for something to erupt, to rip apart the film of inertia covering the town. It was like standing on a high bridge and feeling the creature inside you who wants to throw herself off. But as we stood there waiting, listening to the sound of the E4, I felt as though I had been shot through with light, with inordinate happiness, and I thought I would always have his electric breathing beside me. That didn't happen. Hunter disappeared and I stayed. Sometimes I think we actually knew it would be like that, but also that our destinies were intertwined for a moment, and that is what friendship is, sharing destiny for a time. In that moment it looks as if you are one and the same and that your lives will move in a single direction. I can see all the people I have been friends with in my life, relatively few, but how close we were, always heading the same way, never imagining life would become so different for us all. And no-one has ever been as close to me as Hunter, not even my ex-husbands, no-one comes near to what we had. And yet there was still no sex, at least not in the way I have come to know the rules of that particular game. Certain things happen so early in life, and you think it is just a beginning, but in fact it is the end of something, because there won't be any more to come. Those I truly loved, I loved too soon, and since then something inside me has drained away and I have lived my life in first gear.

The roar of the falls has been silenced now, and there is just the tentative trickle of a little brown stream where once there was the surge of a foaming torrent. The factories are silent too, standing as a reminder of all that went before, like a sleeping behemoth next to the mountain. Sometimes, when I walk past on my way home from work, I notice it is almost four o'clock and inside me I hear the siren that sounded when the first shift was over, and the shadows of all those who once worked there walk beside me for a while before they dissolve into the intense light. I see the slender figure of Hunter's father in his work overalls, before his silhouette fades away. And I see Hunter, a vision coming across the square in his little denim jacket, a German Shepherd at each side. The dogs look like royalty, gliding along beside him, terrifying yet cuddly at the same time. The Smedsby park looks the same as ever. New dogs trample over the lupins, children climb around in the playground as if it's their job.

We wandered about in the wreckage of Ryhov, the old mental hospital, amid broken windows and dilapidated facades and grounds that had grown wild. Inside, along the abandoned corridors, we rode on our skateboards and collected things that had been left behind, mirrors and medicine bottles and scalpels and tins, abandoned as if someone had left the place in great haste. Later they built a new hospital, and I worked there for a short time. Hunter had kept some of the dogs shut in a room on the third floor of the old hospital. He showed me the locked room that was now their home. They were lying together in a big heap on the floor, dozing. When he opened the door, they jumped up and leaped towards him, one form suddenly transformed into ten living bodies, and started running around the room, yelping. It was as if he held life itself imprisoned inside that room, anaesthetised somehow, and as soon as the door opened they began to live again and breathe and reach for the outside world. We took them out into the grounds and they followed Hunter obediently, dachshunds and poodles and massive brown dogs like bears, as if he kept them all on an invisible leash, a bunch of souls that only lived for his visits.

As we walked down the street one day, Hunter's father was standing in his dressing gown, smoking a cigarette, in front of the house next to the community centre. I didn't know that was where they lived, had never asked, just assumed they lived outside town because Hunter sometimes slept in our basement.

"Won't you come in, ladies and gentlemen?"

"Are we allowed?" I said.

I looked around the apartment, room by room. I doubt anyone imagined these rooms actually existed. There were weapons all over: small arms and pistols from Abyssinia and Jakarta and the factory here. Hunter's father sat in an armchair, following us with his gaze.

"I don't know why I've collected all this. You can't take anything with you where I'm going, anyway."

"Where are you going?" I asked, and he laughed as if it was a stupid question, and it was. He pulled on a pair of council regulation trousers under his dressing gown, his complexion sallow against the bright burgundy of the bathrobe.

The last time I went with Hunter to the dogs' room at Ryhov, a giant grey creature emerged from the sleeping pile. I could see immediately it was a wolf and for the first time with Hunter I was scared. It was gaunt and looked frozen and was faster than the others. I was actually afraid of the dogs too, but I never told him. I ran down the stairs and sat on the visitors' bench to wait and I lit a cigarette butt I had brought with me. We had started smoking now, mostly for something to do. When Hunter came down with his great entourage, he didn't see me sitting on the bench, and I watched them go off into the forest. I didn't dare to go with him after that.

One evening we were at my house, watching a video and eating popcorn. It was set in Salt Lake City and we laughed at how similar it was to here: the same inky black mountains closing in on everything. In the middle of the film Hunter suddenly stood up and went out through the porch doors. I followed him. It was warm outside, the grasshoppers were chirping, and when I ran off between the houses it felt like moving through warm water. I raced across the gardens and down towards the waterfall. In the distance I saw Hunter disappear into the moonlight mist. A few days later I saw him from afar with the wolf, as if the two of them were floating along, Hunter with his baggy, oversized trousers and the wolf with its shabby, worn-out coat. I remember thinking that neither of them fitted in here, that the landscape couldn't quite stomach either of them. It was the last time I saw him.

At school his seat was empty and I went round on the way home and took the lift up to their apartment. No-one answered the door and I shouted through the letterbox. A sweet smell came out of it and I could tell from the silence there was nobody there. The new telephone directories were next to the door. His father was sitting outside the Rosen Hotel holding court, and I went up to him and sat down.

"Where's Hunter?"

"You know better than me. It's been a long time since I could keep tabs on things like him."

"Do you know he has a wolf now?"

He laughed. "No-one knows the first thing about boys."

It must have been several weeks later when someone rang the police. Maybe in those days it wasn't such a big thing as it is now if someone disappeared, and two other children had already gone missing. Little Martin was the first, and then the girl. People were afraid, as if ogres were prowling around our small town, and we all knew it could happen to us. A madwoman had claimed responsibility, said she was to blame for everything that had happened to the two children. She had an air of the Messiah about her and I suppose she just wanted to be punished for something, anything at all. The dead children were archived eventually and Hunter forgotten about, as if he had never existed. Perhaps this town couldn't cope with any more disappearances. And Hunter's father had decided to give his child his freedom.

"I trust him to do what he has to do. If he wants to come back, he will. And if he doesn't, well . . ."

His words trailed away, dissolved, and Hunter hurtled into the darkness and was gone.

They closed the factory and something changed. The whole town had relied upon the arms industry, like a fence to lean on. My parents moved away, and if they ever came back to visit me, they looked around in puzzlement, as if they had truly suppressed the memory of this little town where my entire childhood had unfolded. The Atheists had never really belonged here, they moved on in their lives, they went

21

their separate ways, and I stayed here by the waterfall, and then it too fell silent. Every time my parents paid a visit, they laughed at the fact I had stayed in the town. They would arrive together, even though they were no longer married. Perhaps they didn't fancy coming alone. My dialect amused them, and I felt like one of John Bauer's old trolls next to them, their bustle, their cool, unfamiliar scent, their sophisticated gestures. I think most people spend their whole life in the same place, even the ones who move around; I am the same person now as when I was born, it doesn't matter where I live.

Inside me I can still hear the waterfall. When I go and stand there for a while, staring at the dry, desolate mountain, I feel a movement within me, pulling me like a wave before it is halted by time. It is so strong, relentless, surging, and yet so absent. Time blows through us like a wind, and when I look at my body in the mirror, I am time: the heavy hips that used to be thin and bony, my face a parody of the face it once was.

Hunter's father was borne away to the churchyard and new people took over his throne in the town centre. I had been to school with some of them, but they never possessed the same brilliance and grandeur as Hunter's father. They looked tired and always angry. I went to Hunter's father's grave a few times and found flowers there on each occasion, and I would turn to look at the pine trees at the edge of the churchyard, hoping that Hunter would be there.

Every now and then I sit down with them to say hello, but we never have much to talk about.

"Anything going on?"

"Nothing."

He is the one from the class above me who is always heading somewhere with his bags, but that is how people are around here, all the time, en route to somewhere else.

"Weren't you going to Stockholm?" I ask.

"Maybe next year."

"Stockholm's not going anywhere," we say in the same breath.

Then we laugh, because we both know that neither of us will get further than Axamo Airport. I used to take the plane from there as a child. With a little label around my neck, I used to take off and fly out into nothingness and come back home a few weeks later. The air stewardesses were like angels, escorting me onto the aircraft and sitting there, smiling, temporarily strapped in as we climbed through the clouds. I visited numerous relatives and afterwards it was as if those same relatives and their homes didn't exist, they were just a dazzling blur before we descended again to the map of Småland.

"They're rebuilding everywhere," I offer, for something to say. I am thinking of the huge shopping centre that landed like a spaceship in the middle of everything old. And I am ashamed when I think of who I am, even though I have never been anyone special.

"Are they?"

"Yeah, the whole lot. It all has to be new now."

"Christ almighty!"

When you come from the north you see Lake Vättern open out like a shimmering ice-blue ocean. I have never seen anything like it anywhere, and when the light strikes the rear-view mirror, I think I am in Los Angeles, that this is my Los Angeles. I drive the whole distance fast, with an anticipation that won't be fulfilled, but is in me every time, as if life begins right there. The feeling subsides after Tokeryd, where the world appears to shrink and seems to be sucked into a black sack. And I am met by the high mountains that have swallowed the little community, by the blue-lit neon crosses and by the person I am and always have been. It is more than coming home, it is about becoming who I am, whoever that might be, but in some way it is connected to this town with all its facets, its limitations,

A vague sense of being chosen, of arriving and at the same time going wrong. When I drive past the hospital on the way home, I feel it like a longing that never properly passes: a longing to go back to the way it was before, to not have a life of my own, to be at the start of something undiscovered, to not know what will become of me.

THE WHALES

Once, when my mother was a child, she saw a blue whale. It was in an exhibition in the Slaughterhouse district, in the days when dead whales still went on tour. She went with her father and thousands of other Stockholmers who also wanted to see the whale. It had been transported from the North Sea in an articulated lorry and it had started to smell somewhat, a mixture of rotting and formaldehyde. It had been scooped out and was suspended by means of steel cables and crossbars. People waited in a long queue to climb up and walk around inside, where hanging lanterns illuminated the grey flesh, and its ribs formed the ceiling and walls into a small hall. When she and Grandfather stepped into the mighty maw, for a moment they were alone in the world, as if voyaging into the depths of an ocean or the far reaches of empty blackness in space, before they were waved out through an opening in the whale's tailfin by the stressed whale-keeper. When she emerged into the spring light she immediately ran to the back of the queue to enter again. She had to go back in, there was something about the smell and the giddiness it induced, as if a creature inside her had woken up and gradually started to wriggle and writhe. But it was late in the day and almost dusk by then, and the tickets were sold out, and the whaleman was tired and wanted to go to sleep in his lorry.

She wasn't one to ask for things, she never did, she would rather do what was asked of her, sometimes before she was bidden, but the next day she sat beside the post box, waiting for Grandfather to come home from work. When he got off the bus she ran up and whispered to him that she would never again in her life ask for anything if she could just be allowed to return to see the whale. She offered all her remaining pocket money and to comb his hair every evening in front of the wireless. My grandfather was thrifty, they lived modestly and prudently, he worked hard, looked out for discounts and kept accounts, and taking trips to look at whales was not something he was in the habit of doing. The fact that they ended up there in the first place was surprising, but he had seen an advertisement in the newspaper and decided that his daughter should have the chance to see something that was not of their world, something so immense, so measureless and breathtaking, that the very idea of it was impossible to grasp. For some unknown reason, perhaps because she had never asked him for anything before, he said yes, and they dressed up one more time and took a clattering tram to the other side of town.

They saw the whale from a distance, lying there in the swarm of people like a stranded god, at once both demeaned and exalted, and there was something almost pornographic about it, something deeply outrageous. The eyes were imploring and still full of life. She went up close to one of them while they stood in the queue: it was ice-blue and the huge pupil made it look friendly and slightly afraid. It was so alone, the eye, in the middle of all the dead, discarded meat. This time candyfloss and popcorn were for sale outside and a man with a barrel organ was standing next to the whale, turning the handle. The whaleman tore the tickets with an expression of weariness on his face.

Inside the whale they stood in silence. Grandfather, in his Sunday suit, cleared his throat, feeling it was appropriate to say something weighty and prodigious that she would never forget. Finally he said:

"It'll get better, little one, you'll see. Your life won't always be like this."

"Do you think so?" She looked at him.

The light inside was grey too and the stench so intense and heady, she felt as though she was going to fall over.

"No, a new age will come."

"What's it going to be like?"

"What?"

"The age you were talking about."

She also wanted to ask if he thought she was always going to be fat, but he had run out of words now, and he made a rather haphazard bow, as if addressed to her and the whole of Creation, took her hand and walked out of the whale. Grandfather had started out long ago as an errand boy. From the age of twelve he had sprinted up and down staircases all over town with copious packages and items of correspondence. Now he was head of his department in a large firm; quite how it happened he never understood, and since a leopard never really changed its spots, he constantly had to resist the instinct to bow and scrape to everyone he met. Sometimes it was a barely noticeable move of his large head as it fell forward slightly before he remembered to pull it back. Occasionally he would bow to Grandmother when he entered her room, though there wasn't much ceremony left between them.

Next time she went on her own to the Slaughterhouse district. Asking to go for a third time didn't even enter her mind. She packed a suitcase with her clothes, her comics and her boomerang. She took the same tram they had taken last time, but she ended up on the other side of town, as she was not yet old enough to know it was important which side of the road you boarded the tram. After standing at Mariehäll and looking at the reflection of the Marabou factory in the river without knowing what it was, she did what she had read you could do in an emergency: she hitched a lift. A taxi driver picked her up. She had no money, but that didn't matter, he said in his Finland Swedish. He smelled slightly of vodka, like Grandmother, and she sat bolt upright in the back, watching the city go past outside. She told him she was going to see a whale. He smiled in the rear-view mirror.

"Well, well, well! A whale! And where exactly did you think you'd find it?"

"It's at the Slaughterhouse," she said.

"Are you sure you don't want to go to the zoo?"

"Quite sure."

He laughed at her, but drove her where she wanted to go.

He leaned out of the car window as she walked in under the blue Slaughterhouse sign.

"Are you sure you know where you're going, my little cherub?"

"Of course I do."

She had no idea, but she thought she would recognise the smell when she came close. She also knew that, if she got the chance, she would follow that little troupe of one dead whale and one grumpy young man anywhere in the world. The sun was already low in the sky, but no-one would miss her at home for some time: Grandmother would be sleeping it off behind her bedroom door all afternoon as usual. She walked around the entire district for a long time without finding the whale. The place was bigger than she had thought, like a small town. After peeping for a few minutes at some women in blood-spattered aprons who were standing outside the gut room having a cigarette, she plucked up the courage to approach them and ask.

"Oh, that thing," they said, as if to them it wasn't in the least remarkable for a blue whale to lie tipped on its side on the back of a lorry in the Slaughterhouse district. But then, they were looking death in the eye every day. They told her that the whale and the whaleman had gone on their way, no-one knew where; he was a good-looker, but a bit too scruffy for their taste, they said, making the sign of the cross as if on some secret cue. One of them offered her a cigarette, which she declined, then she changed her mind and accepted it, laying it at the top in her suitcase. And eventually she found the place where the lorry had been standing, some forgotten popcorn on the grey asphalt the only sign of the whale and the whaleman. There she stayed until it was dark outside. On the way out she ran straight into the taxi driver, sitting in the driver's cab with the light on, reading a newspaper. He drove her home through the city in silence.

Grandfather was sitting on the step waiting for her when she climbed out of the taxi. He had always said that if she was faced with a lifechanging decision, she should make the brave choice. His eye followed the black car as it slid away down the street. She sat next to him with her suitcase and laid her head on his arm.

"Are you tired?"

"A bit."

"Well, that's to be expected when you've been on the run. Shall we go in and see if we can find something in my encyclopaedia?"

He had acquired a twenty-volume encyclopaedia for an unspeakable sum of money (he may have been duped to a certain degree by the salesman), the likes of which he had never paid for anything before, apart from the house. They didn't have a car either, always travelled by bus or train or tram, Grandfather still maintaining the opinion well into the '70s that the motorcar was a passing craze. Every page had been dipped in gold and when you leafed through the book rays of golden light sprayed out of it, and at night, when the others were asleep, he sat on the veranda and stole into science and history like a thief. He searched for her future in there, imagining that one day she would appear in an illustration of some kind. Sometimes he would sound out new suggestions.

"But of course, you're the Naiad!"

"Or are you Nightingale?"

"Othello . . .?"

"Enid Blyton?"

"Earth mother . . . Aviator . . . Inventor . . . Florist?"

And every time he came to a whale in the alphabet, he shouted for her to come and he read it aloud to her. There was the Antarctic white whale, and their own blue whale, the cachalot, the grey whale, the humpback whale and the minke, the orca and the Pacific whale and several kinds of porpoise. There could be years between whales, and every time she had grown a little bigger. She never saw the blue whale again; she looked for it in the newspaper but she never found it.

"Do you remember when we stood inside the whale's belly?" he asked her each time, as if to reassure her that he knew what she was going through.

*

My mother always longed to get away. From the very beginning she was convinced she was some sort of changeling, that one day this wrong would be righted and she would be returned to her true heritage and her real parents. In the afternoons after school she flopped onto the floor outside Grandmother's bedroom, waiting for her to come out. She would call through the door, scared and at the same time hopeful. Very occasionally there would be a rustle behind the door, it would fly open and Grandmother would storm out like the genie from the lamp, frantic, dishevelled, eyes like a ghost's. But most often there was only silence, and in there the woman in bed had slipped into a different moment in time where the only daughter in the world was herself. The time that prevailed outside the door passed infinitely slowly. It was a graveyard time, a dead time, in which the gilt clock seemed to have frozen mid-stroke. Grandfather often came home late from the office, but when he did it was as if a different world sprang up around them, a sunken Atlantis that suddenly came back to life. Grandmother opened her door and staggered out to the stove, swaying as she prepared something for them to eat, and then the three of them sat at the table with some bread and sausage and tried, each in their own way, to understand how they had wound up here.

*

Their house stood right next to the Råstasjön lake. After the blue-whale outing she spent more and more time down in the sludge of the mudflat with whatever was there: pink stones and mussels and quivering foam. And with what lived further out: a broken seahorse, a forgotten life in a half-open shell, fishes' shadows in the cloudy water, the remains of a beaver's lodge beneath some drowning trees. Like a lone catfish she slid slowly along the bottom behind her yellow goggles, a gift from Grandfather when he reached the word *Diver* in his encyclopaedia. The bottom was wrinkled and shimmering grey below her and the dirty-brown water, harmless little waves constantly reshaping it, and a child could live out a whole life here, pervious like a sponge, without thoughts, without aim. No-one kept an eye on her there. Grandmother lay in bed cursing her fate, or sat in her wobbly camping chair on the veranda staring accusingly at the sky on the other side of the lake. Sometimes in the early evening after work Grandfather sat for a while, marvelling at her somersaults out in the lake, before he called her in. In the distance they were demolishing the Hagalund district, the cranes slow and menacing on the horizon. Later, the blue high-rise buildings would rear up, six powder-blue Atlantic steamers that looked as though they were about to sail off into the future, but by the time they were in place the little swimmer was far away.

*

People say that whales can cure illness, and in the days when dead whales toured the country, people often took along their sick relatives. They carried them through the huge leviathan's corpse and let them touch the dead flesh: fathers and mothers with emaciated, terminally ill children in their arms, the deformed and injured who hadn't been out for years. All these people were hoping for miracles, something that would change the direction of their destinies. The whales slowly rotted as they travelled the roads, and when they could no longer be exhibited, they were thrown back into the sea, filled with all those mortals' impossible dreams, which sank to the bottom with them. When my mother was seventeen, Grandmother suddenly stopped drinking. No-one knew why and it was too late anyway, but nevertheless, she rose from her drunken bed, went into the kitchen, poured away the wine and got the deposit back on all the empties. And from then on that was the road she followed, the straight and narrow, as they called it in those days. The woman I came to know as my grandmother was not the same as the one for whom my mother had waited for so many years outside a closed bedroom door. That harsh, bedraggled creature had submerged somewhere inside her and was entombed there. She was gentle with children and with the stray cats and hedgehogs and mangy foxes and rats she fed in her garden every evening. Grandfather was always quite stern with her: if I ever asked her anything he would always say she didn't know very much about things outside their home, that she'd never read a book in her life, he said it would be best if I asked him when it was something important, and Grandmother smiled and looked down at her hands: her nails were yellow with nicotine and hard as beaks. There had been a time he had stayed with her when she didn't deserve it, and there had also been a time she had stayed with him when she had wanted to leave. She had continued to be his wife and started drinking instead, perhaps to quell her thirst to see the world. And now they were old and approaching death side by side.

My mother never forgave Grandmother, but maybe she was happy all the same to see the two of us bending over one of Grandmother's crosswords, trying to find the words together under the curl of smoke from her menthol cigarette.

"Little mouse," Grandmother said fondly, as she cut her pack of cards, and went on to suggest we play Beggar-my-neighbour. That was also the way she started the winter letters she wrote to me. *Dear little mouse . . . I hope you're well . . . and your mother too . . . I bet she's working as hard as the Almighty himself . . . she's always been so clever . . . so intelligent and quick . . . she's such a bright light . . . and I think you will be too one day . . .*

I followed her shadow between the rhubarb leaves in their garden and through the bracken into the large pine forest next to their house. Her halo of white hair shone in the last of the sunlight and after all those hours in the sun her skin was soft and smooth as silk. She was small and round and a pair of thin brown sundried legs stuck out from under the flowery housecoat she invariably wore, always wet with dishwater. Later, when Grandmother was dying, I kept vigil at her bedside. I rang several times from the hospital and asked my mother to come, but she was at home, lying on the sofa, listening to the gold clock Grandfather had left her . . . *tick, tock . . . tick, tock . . .* and waiting for the last seconds of Grandmother's life to slip away without her. I pretended I was her, sitting there, chatting to Grandmother, because I thought she would be the one Grandmother longed for now that she was about to float out into the great emptiness: her mouth was wide open and black, a hole straight into death. After my grandmother had died, my mother came up to the hospital and looked at her. Grandmother lay like a photograph of herself, staring into eternity, a rose on her breast. She didn't touch her. Maybe she was afraid of her mother even in death.

*

My mother was the first in our family to be awarded her school-leaving certificate. It was such a huge moment for Grandfather, the day she came out into the light on the school steps with twenty other girls; his eyes filled when he saw her in her white student cap and he had to look away. He had searched for her in his encyclopaedia for many years and he still didn't know what would become of her, but there she stood now, about to embark on her life. His school-leaving gift to her was all the golden volumes he had finished reading. They were on our bookshelves when I was a child, the gilt lettering sparkling in the sun's rays as you walked by. On one of our subsequent moves they were taken to the tip. In the photographs from that early-summer day Grandmother is standing beside him in a brown winter coat and felt hat, looking slightly awkward, as if blinded by the bright light, out of place amid all the joy. My mother had already met my father at this stage, he was waiting for her too, somewhere in the shadows, and by now she was slim: one day she had awoken as Orlando and shed her first body and her first self, leaving the old one on the bedroom floor like a twist of peeled-off nylons. She embarked on life as a rather more weightless version. Grandfather and my father would grow to loathe one another. Perhaps Grandfather could smell disaster around him even then, but my father and Grandmother recognised each other immediately as people originating long ago from the same tribe, knowing instinctively they were one and the same kind. I often think of my grandmother's strength of will, getting out of bed one day, clearing up the bottles and vomit, and then never drinking again. Maybe she did suffer a relapse in her loneliness, but each time she must have risen the next morning and faced her grey dishwater. A gift to her daughter that she could never accept. Perhaps she didn't realise it was for her.

My mother swam competitively as a young girl. I don't know how many miles around the earth she covered before she stopped. She always wanted to be close to water and every so often she took herself off on her own to the sea or to a forest lake just so that she could vanish down into the darkness for a while. Sometimes she didn't swim at all, but floated like a water lily on the black water, half sea-nymph, half mother. She used to tell me about a boy in New Zealand who had been brought up by whales. He was only six when he was separated from his parents: they were having a beach party that got a bit out of hand, and when they and their friends moved on to the bars in town, he was left behind by the ocean. All he had was the little Hawaiian garland around his neck and a pair of red swimming trunks. When night began to fall he walked out into the waves to look for them, because he thought that was where they had disappeared, and in a way it was true: they had floated away on a glittering sea of piña colada and sweet-smelling tropical coconut oil, in which they had lost both themselves and him. In the twilight, with the salt waves filling his mouth, he came across a whale family and joined them, and the whales reared him as if he were one of their own. During this time in the Pacific Ocean he would always stay close to the mother whale's huge eye, where she could watch over him, and he could sleep for a while in the light from her eye, while they travelled mile after mile through an underwater world. When he returned from the sea as a sixteen-year-old, no-one recognised him. The mother whale had been killed by a whaler and dragged up onto land, and the rest of the whale family had split up on her death, and when he told people about his life with the whales, they carted him off to the nearest mental hospital and locked him up. He gave the name he had had long ago, but no-one in his first family could believe that this strange youth from the sea had anything to do with their missing six-year-old.

"Did he really follow the whales?" I asked her every time she told me the story.

"Definitely."

I could see the boy before me, locked away in Seacliff Mental Hospital at the point where the southern Pacific meets the Antarctic Ocean, I saw his face just beneath the salty surface. I looked at my mother's face, at the veil that was always there, drawn over her secrets, and I saw my grandmother's face there too, like a quivering double in the ocean mirror.

"But how could he live under water for so long?"

"Because he had to."

I believed her every time, knew instinctively it was an ability I too would need some day: you held your breath and sank down into the water, your lungs were aching and it might last for years, but you had to do it. I thought of Janet Frame's advice from Seacliff. *Don't struggle if you would be rescued from drowning. Never sleep in the snow. Hide the scissors.*

"Would I be able to do it too?" I asked.

"Of course you would."

When I was a child we used to wander around the whale skeletons in the Natural History Museum in Gothenburg. My mother worked as senior consultant at Lillhagen Psychiatric Hospital and we lived at the edge of Slottsskogen park. I always imagined it was the dead whale family from New Zealand we were staring at.

"You're not allowed to touch them," she said, and then did so herself. When she thought I wasn't looking she traced a line with her finger along the gigantic bleached-white rib and went up so close her lips must have brushed against it. I thought about the whaleman she had never seen again, about the person she would have become if she had gone with him all that time ago. There was a cool primordial breeze blowing through those rooms, a heavy redolence of fossils and a bygone age, an odour bound up with the earth's creation, with the volcanos and great ice caps, with the plants and animals that settled into the rock and were turned to stone. There was a sensation of such extreme motion it made your head spin, walking around in there made you hungry for life. When I gave birth to my first child, the whale aroma came back to me. My baby smelled as if he came straight out of a prehistoric ocean, an odour that instantly made you want to give up your own life and do anything for a tiny, unknown swaddle. Lying on the narrow hospital bed, looking at him while the New Year fireworks whizzed up into the sky, I had a strong sense that my life was over. It didn't matter if I died, I thought, because he was the one who was going to live now, and I saw myself as the shell he left behind him, a gleaming chrysalis whirling away into black space.

LONE STAR STATE

He would never forget his delight when Bill rang, and after that the bus journey to Houston, while Hazel slept against the window and he was on his own to watch the stream of industry and forest flash past. The bus was almost empty, as was the landscape outside. It was a night without end, a USA that unfurled into eternity around them. They had no idea who the man was who called himself their father, only that he was wealthy and powerful and that they would be able to work in one of his companies. He had contacted them after all these years, as if no time at all had passed, and in his rather strangled, hoarse voice, ordered them to come. This was where the world began, next to the multi-lane highways, and it was where Bill had once disappeared; it had been no big deal and a long time ago. Bill had been distant and kept himself to himself all the time he lived with them, and his interest had been mostly in Lana. His things were littered around the house for a while afterwards, shirts and shoes and assorted newspapers no-one bothered about anymore, but in time they too disappeared, swept away by new things that had arrived in the little house. And now that Bill was back in their lives, Robin and Hazel weren't sure they would recognise him. They had studied Lana's few photographs of him intently and tried to memorise every trait. What if he'd shaved off his moustache? How would they recognise him then? The evening before they set off he rang to check they were coming and Robin asked:

"Just one thing, Bill. I wanted to ask. Do you have a moustache?"

Bill only laughed and continued to tell him about the oil field burning at night that made Texas look like Armageddon.

"But do you? Still have a moustache? We're kinda afraid we won't recognise you."

He laughed again. "Of course you'll recognise your old man! Can I talk to sexy Lana?"

"Yes. OK," Robin said, wondering how that was going to work out. They were given the address of a bar where he would be waiting for them. He could picture loads of people like Bill in a place like that, and they'd be weaving their wheelie bags between the tables and then go and approach the wrong man.

*

Once they did finally walk in through the shining glass doors, there was only one person in the entire place and he looked exactly like Lana's old photograph. A thick moustache and a wild grin that divided his face, and when he stood up and came towards them he seemed huge. Later he would shrink, it was only in the bar he was so enormous. As they stood there with their bags, looking at him, he was remarkably familiar, on account of the photos no doubt. He instructed them to sit down and ordered hamburgers with pickles for them, and then watched them in awe while they ate, as if they were a couple of weird characters who had just turned up in his life from nowhere.

"How's hot Lana?" he asked, but they couldn't think of an appropriate reply. It is fair to say they were more or less struck mute in his presence, and their mother seemed more done in than hot, but what did they know of the ways of lust? That's right, zilch. They watched Bill surreptitiously while they waited for him to tell them what was going to happen next. They wolfed down their hamburgers because they thought he was in a hurry, but when they had finished eating he sat smoking and staring out of the window at the gas pumps outside. They felt like little children again, and looked silently at the pumps with him.

*

Then he started to speak, half to himself and half to them, and maybe a little to the staff, on whom he was keeping an eye the whole time.

"This is a real dump of a town, but I've done well. Everyone knows who I am. As you'll discover when you tell people you're related to me."

He fell silent and retreated into himself. They glanced at one another. It looked as though he had tuned out completely and forgotten they were sitting there, waiting for him to say something about their future and why he had summoned them. His mind seemed to have vacated that enormous body and left it empty and deflated, and was possibly wandering around the gas pumps outside now.

Then suddenly he rose to his feet and walked towards the door.

"We can't sit here all day. You don't think you've come here for a holiday, do you?"

And with that he was gone. They grabbed their wheelie bags and rushed after him. Bill was sitting in a gigantic jeep, impatiently rapping a finger against the steering wheel as if he had been waiting for them for hours.

"What sort of work are we going to do?" asked Hazel, the bold one of the two.

"Gasoline."

"OK. Are we going to live with you?"

"Yup. There's just me and the Dogs."

The Dogs were four teenagers from Rimini who floated around the house serving hamburgers and lemonade and mango. They did the washing and scrubbed the floors, and when they were free they watched videos with Bill or flopped out by the pool, as if the sun rendered them unconscious. They would sometimes raise their heads and look around, before sinking back into their daze. They spoke only to Bill; he whistled for them like dogs when he came home from work. When they caught sight of Robin and Hazel, they giggled and started whispering to each other. They never addressed them directly, and when they tried to say something themselves, all they received in return was a murmured aside. A faint odour of teenage sweat hung around them all the time, honeybees and bumblebees flew up and down overhead, and sometimes a little jet plane whizzed across the sky over the pool.

Each morning, Robin and Hazel accompanied Bill in his car to the oilfield, but after a few hours someone on the staff would send them home again to spend the rest of the day with the Dogs. They loafed around in the office without any proper duties, and looking back much later Robin supposed they had been summoned there as a diversion, to protect the secrecy surrounding the Dogs.

"Say hello to my kids, they're here for the summer," Bill might shout when anyone passed through the office, and then they had to shake hands and kowtow, but otherwise he didn't speak to them. He seemed to view them as entertaining oddities who had turned up in his fancy life with their frayed jeans and caps and shabby bags, things which appeared even shabbier in Bill's gleaming house. Sometimes he scratched his eyebrow and stared at them.

"So when are you leaving?"

They looked at one another and then at Bill.

"We don't know."

"You don't know much. How are you going to manage in life, have you considered that?"

"Aren't we going to work for you?"

"Yeah, sure. But you have to have a plan for your life. You can't bank on me fixing everything for you."

At night they lay by the pool in the moonlight, talking about when they could go back. They were homesick for Lana. Now they missed everything they had taken for granted about her, her dirty apron and the wet washing dripping all over the house. Yet they didn't want to give up and go home. They had a feeling something was waiting for them here, something was going to happen, there was a reason they had been summoned. It was as if they could smell the disaster that was about to befall them, but mistook it for something else. Bill continued to observe them as if he didn't really understand who these people were who were lounging around his house. Then he locked himself in with the Dogs and watched videos.

They had escaped to their bedroom with a telephone.

"What do you think Lana's doing?"

"Sleeping."

"Shall we wake her?"

Lana wheezed into the receiver, her voice croaky with sleep.

"Is that you, my little wurzels?"

"We want to come home."

She rustled around in the bed with the phone and they could picture her with curlers in her hair and her face shiny with cream.

"Well, come home then."

"Can we?"

"Just take the bus. I'll make chicken curry. Get a move on!"

But days passed and Hazel wanted to stay a little longer.

"I can sense something's going to happen."

It was like the advertising slogan for the doomed plane

that crashed into a mountainside in Nevada. *If you're looking for a great surprise, come fly with us.*

Hazel had stood in front of the mirror that last evening, staring into it as though transfixed. Robin lay in bed watching her, fascinated by her interest in herself. He envied her this. His own face aroused nothing at all in him, he could be anyone: kind of handsome, kind of ugly, nothing particularly distinctive about his appearance whatsoever. He looked like Bill, according to everyone at work at least. Hazel looked like Lana, according to Lana.

"What are you searching for in there?"

"Uh! It always goes wrong," Hazel said, tossing her head. The flip she had been working on all afternoon swayed at the back. He thought she looked prettier without the hairdo. She always looked pretty. Too pretty to be lying in the cemetery with earth in her eyes, as she would be soon.

It was to this moment he would always return later, the moment when she looked at him in the mirror with one eye inky with liner and the other one bare, and said that she really wanted to go back.

"I miss Dad."

She gazed at her own reflection in surprise and clapped her hand over her mouth.

"I mean Mom!"

They laughed at the idea that someone could miss Bill.

"We'll go as soon as you want," he said. "I don't think he'll even notice we've gone."

Muffled noises were heard from Bill's TV room upstairs, the sound of the Dogs' contrived anything-for-a-visa titters.

"Would you like some company tonight?" he asked, when her night incarnation emerged.

"Definitely not!"

And with that and a flick of her hair, she swirled out into the night. After she had gone, he went out too and drifted around aimlessly. He had taken something to pass the time and he took a bit more to keep awake. It was like walking through deep snow even though it was summer. He checked in his pockets to see if they had snow in them, and when the moon rose over the town he walked into a stranger's garden and lay down on a sunbed to bask in the moonlight.

He was asleep in bed, in that slumber special to certain dreams: a black wave that welled up inside him, bore him away, buried him for an instant. The sound of a telephone ringing, or maybe it was a woman crying, filtered in through the blackness pressing down, and he was swimming up to the shimmering surface high above. These were the last seconds before he knew: the darkness of the dream through which he swam and the light above. Naked, he sat up in bed, wrapped himself in a blanket and shuffled towards the thin screen door.

"May I come in?"

It was an elderly police officer waiting for him outside, with the sun at his back and glistening eyes. He told it like it was, there was no point in dragging it out. After that Robin sat on the sofa in front of the policeman with the Saint Bernard eyes, and a storm howled inside him. And then he was in the room alone, and alone he would always be from now on.

They caught Faye the same day. She was still high, she still had the pickaxe in her handbag among the pink lipsticks and old needles. She confessed at once that she had murdered Hazel and said she had no regrets. She spat at the police officers when they questioned her. Perhaps she just wanted to make everything worse, but at any rate she said:

"Do you know I came every time I drove the pickaxe into that girl's chest?"

Robin had travelled home for Hazel's funeral and stayed. Lana was sitting in the hammock, being rocked by the breeze. She looked worn out now, as slender as an ancient birch tree, but her eyes were the same, forever young.

"The older I get, the younger I feel inside," she said. "Today I'm only seventeen."

In her heart Lana was standing on life's threshold again, the age when you can clearly see the world's edges, razor-sharp and unwavering.

Sometimes, when he was surfacing from his dreams, he didn't know whether it was Hazel or him who was dead. He was Hazel then, lying in her grave, crawling with worms. He hadn't heard from Bill since the funeral and hadn't expected to. But nor had he expected him to be stone-dead. There had been hundreds of telephone calls about Hazel, and now there was one more, about Bill: he had been found dead in the big house, half in, half out of bed. Lana laughed out loud when she received the news. She sat in her armchair hooting like a hyena after she had put the receiver down. Robin was lying on the floor and with a guarded smile he watched her howling with laughter, the mint-green telephone still on her knee. He wondered whether she had won on the horses.

"What are you laughing at, Mom?"

She dried her tears and told him that Bill was dead and that someone had sprayed PERVERT on the green wallpaper in his bedroom. Then she erupted again, as if something invisible was shaking her.

"Is that why you're laughing?"

He got up from the carpet and walked out onto the veranda. The clouds looked like an enormous chariot passing across the sky, stark white in the blue.

An assistant from work had gone to Bill's house when he hadn't turned up at the office for a few days, and had discovered him kicked to death in his bedroom. The Dogs were stretched out in the sun by the pool as usual and hadn't seen anything or heard anything, as if utterly consumed with the sunshine and themselves. Robin could picture them from many hundreds of miles away, lifting their lazy heads to the black sun.

"Bill? . . . Oh, yeah, he must be up there asleep, the old grizzly."

For several weeks the Dogs continued to float around the garden in their mini tank tops and cut-off jeans and shiny, cropped haircuts. Then they were arrested. But since they kept giving different accounts during the trial, there was nothing anyone could use to put them away. Those boys were like a four-headed riddle, all their stories were blind alleys. So they were released at the end of the trial and, notwithstanding the numerous versions, there was no-one who could really accept the story about the man with a houseful of Italian teenagers. But, in any event, the small oil empire and the house were sold and a bagload of money was dispatched to Robin and Lana. A will had been found in the house after Bill's murder, and most of the money went to the four lonely boys. Robin could never bring himself to wonder about the will (or anything else concerning Bill), he would never want something (or love something) again, and, for him, he was now rich. He bought a house for Lana in Huntsville, not far from the prison holding Faye. Afterwards he thought that he must have had the notion of getting closer to Hazel even back then.

Over the subsequent years, he was to think a great deal about forgiveness. On the one hand there was stuff that would always blow over, and on the other hand there was the unforgivable. Such as Lana laughing like a hyena: he had already let that go, before she had even stopped laughing. But then there was the fact that Hazel was no longer by his side, with her flip hairdo and her piercing, shining eyes. Since the unforgivable was the only thing there was to forgive, you had to live with the problem for eternity, an engine that started up every morning, an arrow that flew through him forever. Until one day he turned to God, the god that hovered high over Texas and the oil field, the same god that had once made Bill rich. And finally, after several years had passed, he turned to the woman with the pickaxe. He requested a meeting with her, to spit in her face, and because he still didn't know what to do with the rest of his life.

When he entered the visiting room at the prison the first time, Faye had kept absolutely still, not said a word, just stared at him until he lowered his eyes to the floor. He had been told that she had changed during the six years that had passed, that now she was someone else. She had become a believer, and so had he. She sewed clothes for poor children, she had distanced herself from the person she had been before, she had confessed and begged for forgiveness and surrendered to her fate. He didn't care whether she had turned into someone else, hers was still the hand that had taken Hazel from him and that was enough for him. He simply wanted to see her, to have seen her, and then go home and wait for the state to kill her on his behalf.

He didn't know what he had been expecting, a rush of pleas for forgiveness, sobs, or ice-cold denial, but not this numb silence. Finally she said that she'd been waiting for him. And he began to weep. Such was his grief over Hazel that it had had no voice, there had been nowhere to release it, it was too immense, too unwieldy; there was no space for it in the world. This was the first time since her death that the situation and the place seemed able to hold it. When he came back out into the sunshine he had the sense he had been in there for years, the trees and cars and people outside the prison must have been replaced several times over, presidents must have come and gone, wars too.

Lana became sick and didn't want to get well again. They couldn't really find anything wrong with her, but she didn't want to rise in the mornings and she didn't want to stay in her fine new house. The house had shrunk, she said, and she lay down under a pile of blankets in the garden with her eyes closed. Robin dreamed again that he was lying in the coffin beside Hazel. She lay on her side gazing up at him under her inky eyelashes.

"Why can't I come back to you?" she whispered.

He woke up on the floor in Lana's house to the sound of a pickaxe. In the ferocious heat people were constantly hacking away in their refrigerators and freezers. It was so bad in the bars he could no longer go in, to the wonderful, glittering bars that had saved him before. Lana lay naked in the hammock, asleep with her mouth open, and he thought she looked like an old, abandoned baby. He went out and pulled a crocheted blanket over her. The sound of ice being crushed was drowned out by the roar of a lawnmower starting up.

He returned to the prison, and each time he passed the guard tower he would tell himself it was for the last time. As he walked through the building's many doors, it felt like going ever deeper into a dark dream in which he no longer knew who he was. Under the flickering fluorescent light in the furthest corner of the black þuilding, a Christ-like woman sat and sewed, and her naked eyes looked up at him and she said nothing. The silence had a draw to it: he went in and sat down and listened to it, and for the first time since Hazel died he was utterly calm, for the first time in his life he didn't feel pursued. He started visiting Faye and he couldn't stop. Whatever was outside the prison faded, slipped away.

Over the years that followed it sometimes felt as though the room she was in was the only room in the world: the harsh light of the cell transmuting into green, the dark-grey walls, the reek of death and institution. Each time the security guards patted him down he was inwardly at peace. When he was sitting with Faye, wedged into the concrete air pocket called the visiting room – there were no windows, no pictures on the wall – he felt a sense of freedom in not being able to make the slightest movement without someone at the other end of the room putting a hand on their belt. And much later he realised that it made no difference whether Faye was alive or dead, if he spat in her face or not. What had happened would have happened anyway. But if someone in those early years had told him that one day he would sit on the bench for the family of the condemned when she was executed, he would have laughed like Lana did the day Bill died.

It was the woman with the pickaxe, and yet it wasn't her. There was something about time: Faye seemed to float alongside her crime, as if she and the girl with the pickaxe had gradually slid apart, separated into two. Umpteen criminals hid behind their crimes, impossible to glimpse, but the woman with the pickaxe just seemed to have walked away, left her mothership without looking back. And every time he was there he imagined he was coming slightly closer to Hazel, for it was Faye who had touched her, even to the point of death. Sometimes he caught a glimpse of Hazel in her eye, a bobbing hair flip in a pale, unaccountable light. They had their God, that was what they talked about, it was neutral ground. They had both bowed down before him in the end, it was one thing they could agree on: something to submit to, the prayers, the rituals, acknowledging the pain in earthly human lives. Sometimes he wondered what would have happened if they hadn't had that God to unite them, that Bible she held to her chest when he entered the cell.

Lana died. She passed away as quietly as she had lived for the last few years, there was hardly any difference. Over at Glenwood the grave was opened and they lowered her slender body down next to Hazel. When he stood and watched the gravedigger fill the hole with earth, he thought that the only person in the world who wished as fiercely as he did that Hazel would come back was Faye.

For eight years he wanted to kill her, and then he forgave her. It was the most difficult thing he had done in his entire life. It was more difficult than Hazel's death, more difficult than Bill's acts against the boys. Yet he did it. And still Hazel and Faye and Bill and the Dogs lived within him. It was like a war in there, impossible to control them, and whenever he had the recurrent feeling they were fighting each other locked away somewhere deep inside his body, he would run along the streets until he could no longer breathe. What did it matter in the end who had killed whom, and why, when the world was going to end anyway one day? So he gave up. That was when he became free. Well, not free. But he stopped keeping track, he stopped keeping a tally. All he knew was that he didn't want the state to kill her, anything other than more death, and perhaps that was what ultimately drove him to Faye. In contrast to the president, he didn't want to hand over to God the question of forgiveness, he thought it belonged in their world, in the world that had robbed him of Hazel.

*

It was as though eventually he could see Faye behind her crime, as if after all these years it had detached itself from her, like a shadow slinking away from its owner, or someone emerging from a photograph and drifting off. It would obviously be absurd to say that Faye took the place of his dead sister, but maybe somehow that is what happened.

"I love you, Robbie," was one of the last things she said. It might have been an odd thing to say for someone who had hacked his sister to death with a pickaxe, and yet that was how it was. Hazel wasn't there anymore, her death would soon be long ago, and he had lived with it for many years by now. His sister had once been closer to him than anyone else, but everything had hurtled on in the world from which she had been snatched. It was also true that everything that had happened after Hazel's death had changed him, indelibly. He was no longer the same, and in a way he felt lighter than he had ever felt. He had been able to say: "I've never felt as happy as I've been since Hazel died."

Sometimes when he visited Faye he fancied he could see the shadow of the pickaxe girl standing alone in a corner of the cell with her axe, staring at him and Faye. He wondered if he was the only one who could see her. And she was there at the end too. Like a pesky little ghost she fluttered around them to the very last. He wanted to ask her to come and sit next to him so the execution chamber could be calm, but it was too late for that, Lone Star State was finished with Faye, and the girl with the pickaxe would have to leave with her mothership. He could sense her angry presence, the aggressive little current of air through the room when she flew on her way. And just this once, before it too went up in smoke, it occurred to him that it was not the person who had killed Hazel whom he had forgiven, it was the new Faye, someone else entirely. But as he had decided to stop keeping track and keeping a tally, then so be it.

*

Faye's eyes were covered by a black blindfold, but she knew Robin was there, just a few yards from her, and she knew he was there for her, in her final hour. She turned her head and, although inside her darkness, she looked at him, and he reached out and pressed his hand against the glass.

THE VICTORIA WATER LILY

When I was young, she was the only one. The priest's daughter, Evelina. I remember the fragrance around her as if she was still beside me. I can conjure up the odour seeping out from between her legs on those winter afternoons in my room in the middle of the '80s. A slightly musty smell, reminiscent of a hospital, like a baby's unwashed bottom, or powder. Not at all like women I have known since. All the others have had the sweet pungency of musk or standing seawater, but not her. I remember this too: how she believed the heavens would fall every time she was intimate with another girl. She leaped up and with trembling fingers tried to pull together the little tear in my curtain that would always open up and let the blue light in between the ragged threads. "Nobody can see us," I whispered in her ear, fascinated by the strength of her belief that her body was in direct association with the heavens above. I worked on the assumption that heaven paid no attention to our existence, that our brief moment on earth passed unremarked. Evelina was different, her body was in tune with the laws of nature, with God's wrath, with the planets circling around us out there. She claimed she could remember the fall of man, when we had plummeted, wingless. I went along with her on everything, because I was mad about her. Later, when she had been transported to the stars again and was back in bed with me, and heaven had closed around her cuts and wounds, she was, for one instant, defiantly happy, before running home across the motorway beneath the violet evening sky settling on the city. She ran home to the priest by Brunnsviken and confessed everything.

I grew up at the Museum of Natural History. Evelina lived in a villa by the shore of Lake Brunnsviken. We hung out in the old exhibition rooms, where we raced around after all the lights had been turned off, and when we were tired of running, we made love on the floor in one of the cloak-rooms. We would occasionally fall asleep in there and be awoken by the sound of the security guards coming along, their dogs barking. We snatched up our clothes and dashed half-naked back to where I lived in the staff accommodation, the Black Villas, close by. Sometimes when I visit my father in the museum, I can still hear our laughter echoing deep inside the building, and if I screw my eyes up tight I can imagine I see two young girls flying through the rooms like a pair of ghosts from the '80s.

"Do you remember Evelina?" I want to say, but I never do.

Evelina could never lie when she went home to the priest. Everything we had done throughout the afternoon poured out of her when she got there, and when she was back with me the following day and removed her tights, her shins and the backs of her thighs were mottled with blue. I knew I was the cause of the marks, that they would cease the moment I disappeared from her life, but still we carried on meeting. The old marks yellowed and new ones appeared, sharp and brighter, reddish, yellow and brown. I have never been able to conceive that anything I did could give rise to such ferocity. No-one had ever harmed so much as a hair on my head, neither at home nor anywhere else. We never touched one another in our family, no displays of affection or acts of abuse, but there was nevertheless a kind of tranquil love that made me feel secure. Sex was my first encounter with both violence and tenderness, and I often had the feeling that they couldn't be separated. It wasn't that we hurt each other, Evelina and I, it wasn't even the bruises that regularly appeared on her legs and then faded, but I marvelled at the aggression arising between us when we touched, the easy hostility.

"Can't you say you're doing homework with a friend?" I asked, while she lay on my arm in the museum basement, staring up at me. I had pulled down the unclaimed coats and jackets and built a den for us. There was nothing untrue in those clear, sad eyes looking at me as if I could protect her from the world outside. At first I thought she was teasing, but she truly couldn't lie: language and words were like mathematics or physics to her. Lying was like trying to hold back the light.

"If he asks, I just tell him what we've done," she said simply. "I tell him everything. I make him listen to all the details."

The motorway passed between the museum and Brunns-viken and we would stand on either side watching each other, filled with other-worldly longing. Whenever I saw the priest in the distance with his mass of wild hair hovering above his head, I made myself scarce, hiding behind a tree or shrinking down next to a fence. I never went to her house, but I used to stand and spy on them as they slowly moved about their garden, the priest in his overalls and Evelina and her mother in yellow raincoats. From here the whole scene looked quite haphazard, like life itself, while

Evelina's face glowed in the half-light as she threw leaves onto a bonfire. They kept a racing yacht below the house, the nearest I came to being in her home. We slept over there a few times, with me waiting for her at the water's edge until the house was dark, and then her climbing out of her bedroom window and coming down to meet me. The sound of the water lapping against the hull woke us early, the slivers of sky glinting in the narrow windows, the chorus of thousands of birds circling above us. I would hurry home in the pink glow of a dawn that looked like death. Some nights we broke into the botanical gardens and swam out to the Victoria water lily. When it bloomed you could lie inside, like in a nest, the leaves so strong it could hold our weight. Every so often we would be trapped in there when the flower closed up in the morning, us and the many beetles who spent their nights there.

When we moved from the Black Villas – it was around the time I left home and my father lost his job – it transpired that my mother had found her own apartment. In a matter of a couple of weeks we had scattered, the three people who had shared the same home, watched television from the same sofa and used the same bathroom. "I hung on for your sake," she said over a glass of wine at Tennstopet after she had shown me her new, empty lodgings. It was typical of her just to ride things out, it wasn't something I had asked her to do, and it had only made her withdrawn and secretive with me. The museum let my father stay and pick through the collections and catalogues, I suspect because they couldn't actually manage without him. He moved out to student accommodation in Lappis. He is still there in the museum, bent over a jar of formaldehyde, eye to eye with an ancient cuttlefish. I am always filled with a special affection when I see him sitting there. Perhaps animal life is the only thing that has never frightened him.

When we finished high school, Evelina and I lost touch. I started studying at university and she went to some kind of Christian boarding school near Uppsala. We met a few times during the '90s; once she was standing in the rain outside my student room, wanting to borrow an egg, and we saw each other now and then after that. On one occasion she invited me back for dinner in Knivsta to introduce me to her boyfriend. I was curious to know who she had chosen. I could see instantly he was a jerk. He had a friend with him and they spoke only to each other, like little boys at a kids' party. She had laid the table really nicely, with linen napkins and a vase of flowers, even though we were so very young. We were slightly awkward, sitting around the table, fiddling with the big serviettes, and the two of them had fled before we reached the lobster soup. I had gone to the toilet and Evelina was battling with the main course in the kitchen – I knew that sort of thing didn't come naturally to her – and when we came back the chairs were empty. We searched all over the minute apartment, we looked in the stairwell, we even craned our necks out of the window, but they were nowhere. They must have jumped onto one of the local service trains that hurtle into the city every fifteen minutes. Evelina wept into the bisque.

"It was only tinned," I tried.

I didn't yet know what it was like to love in the way she loved that buffoon. I had just wriggled my way out of the cosy captivity of childhood and I still wasn't quite ready to submit to anyone. Evelina was someone whom others would always regard as rather simple; they couldn't see the genius hidden behind a face like hers, behind the clownlike features and the eyes so large and blue she always looked a tiny bit surprised, the hair, thin, wispy and almost white. They didn't appreciate the clarity in her gaze, the vitality in her eyes. On my twentieth birthday she came to the party in Little Red Riding Hood shoes and she had to sleep over when she missed the bus home. It was cold where I lived then and we slept next to each other in long johns and thick socks. After that we went our separate ways out into the world and it would be decades before I saw her again. I heard that she had trained to be a deacon and had lived in Ecuador and Venezuela. She had been the victim of a fraudster somewhere along the line; it had been in the newspaper. I had always considered women who were taken in by that sort of thing as headcases, with their morbid longing to be swept away by diamonds and fine words, but now all I could see before me were her wide eyes which seemed to drink in the world unfiltered. Everything was soaked up and preserved in that tremulous black pupil. As for me, I had thrown myself into science.

The university's main buildings, a stone's throw from the museum, had faded, their sky-blue colour whitened like ancient edifices that had once been vibrantly resplendent. My office was on the eighth floor in one of them. And one Sunday evening when large parts of life had already sailed by, I was standing alone in a banqueting hall under a massive crystal chandelier, waiting to give my talk on Newton – my life's work and my meal ticket, Newton and a few other gentlemen of science – when suddenly Evelina was standing in front of me, as if she had risen out of a hole in the floor. I was always mindful that there might be someone from the past among the audience – there usually was, a classmate or an old boyfriend's aunt. For a while our religious studies teacher from Stora Skuggan would turn up to my lectures drunk. This was different: it was as if my sixteen-year-old self were standing before me.

"So *you*'re here then?" she said quietly, as if we were already in the middle of a conversation. Her voice was still hoarse, slightly croaky.

"Yes," I said, "why *shouldn't* I be here?"

I was irritated. I was the one going to speak this evening, I was the focal point of all this, the cut glass, the big stage, the people milling around, and yet she was surprised to find me here. It was the same with my mother: when once in a blue moon she would come to hear my lecture, she accompanied me to the university across the city, and then she kept pushing me to get a move on, until I finally stopped and snapped, *It's hardly going to start before I get there.* Which she just regarded as arrogance, or pure silliness, and she whacked me with her handbag and hurried off down the street with a firm grip on her lapel. She had been dead for several years now, so it wasn't really an issue; the whole mother-problem had partially receded.

Evelina laughed softly.

"I only meant that I was pleased to see you. It's been hard to imagine you were still here. I've seen you in pictures in the paper and on TV, but it's not the same thing. You seem so serious in those. I don't remember you as serious."

"No, you were the serious one."

We stood in silence and she gently twisted her glass. Her hair was as blonde as before. I looked for grey amidst the golden, but every strand seemed full of light and life even now.

"I didn't know Newton was a virgin. That's why I'm here."

Then she walked away. People were supposed to mingle, but I became distracted by her presence as she went from group to group, saying a few words before moving on. I used to be wary about getting stuck with the same person all evening when I was trying to mix, bored rigid but also wanting to give my all, lost in banal, aimless conversations, incapable of circulating in the room. I always knew in advance what people were going to say, I always wanted to fast forward; it was as if they were all following a badly written, or an exceedingly well-written, script. Frequently I found myself wanting to speed up time, to come to the end, all those thoughts about the future being really just a desire for life to be finally over.

One New Year's Eve I had celebrated the stroke of midnight without my husband, when I managed to get caught on a balcony with another man who seemed lonely and quite abandoned by life. My husband had really chortled about that, how he had been standing on his own with his glass of champagne as the clock struck twelve. Now he too was far away, in Cape Town with our grown-up sons. How

I missed them. The feeling I had known when they were little and I had to go away on a trip and leave them was nothing compared to the feeling I had now, when they would only ever come home again as strangers.

In our last year at high school, Evelina became convinced that she was carrying a baby Jesus. She came running across the motorway to tell me the news. I was flattered that she truly believed I could make her pregnant, but she wept with terror. She laid my hand on her chubby angel's tummy.

"Maybe you've just eaten too much cabbage?" I said.

"I hate cabbage," she said, and wept even more.

"Cake then?"

"It was just like this for the Virgin Mary."

"You're joking, right?"

She was serious as ever.

In the end I took her to a clinic for young girls like us.

"I am definitely in that condition," she said on the way there. "I don't need a doctor to find that out."

"But how?" I asked.

She didn't answer, as people won't when the questions are too stupid.

At the clinic a woman used an imaging machine on her pale stomach, wherein it was dark and silent.

"There's no baby inside you, little one," she said when she had finished. Evelina nodded dutifully, pulled down her top and said she understood. But later when we were sitting on a bench in the park outside, she said:

"At least it'll make Dad happy when he hears there's a little Jesus inside me."

"But listen," I said, forcing her to look at me, "are you crazy? I mean, it doesn't matter if you are crazy, I just need to know."

She said she wasn't, and after a few weeks she let it drop, whatever it was, and it lost its hold over her. When I look back, I think she just needed to engage with it for a while; it was something she had been obliged to do in order to live with the fact of the two of us. It struck me that she and I were slightly alienated from our own species, that we were more at home with my father's extinct great apes sitting around their pretend fire in the depths of the museum, warming themselves to eternity. The sloping forehead, the hairiness, the dull yet watchful gaze, the primitive desire: that was *our* look. Or maybe we were just normal demon kids. When I walked around the collections as a child, I would often look at my father and wonder if he too was an ape under his white coat, he felt so very close to those creatures of old. At night I would search my body for signs that I was a great ape as well: I had a thin tell-tale seam of dark hair running from my pageboy haircut down my back. Evelina would run her finger down the stripe when I lay on my stomach half asleep.

Everybody always loved the idea that Newton was a virgin. Like Joan of Arc, I used to say, and Hans Christian Andersen, and Norman Bates, and Lewis Carroll with his rabbit hole. The day after the lecture, Evelina was waiting for me outside the university when I left. We walked together for a while and, as if it was something we had planned, we ended up in the green darkness of our childhood maze at Belleville. It was spring, the ground was soft and smelled so good, like childbirth.

"Do you want to go in?" Evelina asked, and led the way. I watched the sun's shadows playing on her coat as she walked ahead of me, and I looked down at my feet treading after her as they always had done. In the centre of the labyrinth you were supposed to make a wish, but neither of us had a coin. We had walked in silence most of the way there, apart from me talking a little more about Newton. Forever Newton, if people only knew how tired I was of Newton and his endless scientific squabbles.

"Aren't you going to ask anything about my life?" she said when we were standing in the middle, as a ray of sun danced across her face.

"Of course."

"I'm still a virgin," she said quickly, before I could think of a question. I laughed aloud.

"You're not."

"Yes, I am."

"How can you say such a thing to me?"

"Well, that's what my doctor says, anyway."

She went quiet. I watched the ray of sun gleam in her eye. She was still so beautiful it felt indecent. I thought of the two of us inside the Victoria water lily, the soft pink glow in there, how light we were, how it wouldn't support us now.

"Did you really believe you were carrying Jesus in your stomach back then?"

"I don't know. Maybe. What we had was such a miracle."

"Do you think so?"

"Of course I do."

I didn't need to mention the priest; he was there with us in the labyrinth with his mop of unruly hair and his black eyes. Every time she had returned to me, she had let me stroke the new marks.

"Life has been quite hard on him," she said, her voice mild, almost neutral.

"I'm glad."

She stared at me, her eyes steady and wide open, her pupils dilating.

"Without those bruises I wouldn't have survived. Didn't you understand?"

We left the maze and walked on under the Djurgården oak trees, which stood as they had a hundred years ago, immovable, immortal. We didn't speak, there wasn't much to say, there are no words for the most important thing in life. I had the strong sense of a Rilke moment as I was walking beside her, a feeling I had experienced a few times in my life, and each time my life had changed direction. Once when I had seen a torso of Apollo in the Louvre in Paris and confused him with Icarus, and then I returned to Stockholm and dropped out of the last term of medical school; and once when I had seen a portrait of Isaac Newton and didn't know who he was. I saw myself and Evelina as if from above as we walked along beneath the canopy of trees, swathed in the scent of spring with no idea of who we were or where we were going, as if I were sitting on a star far out in space.

THREE SISTERS

Originally we were three sisters. We were not especially alike, but one of us did resemble our guardian. The same angular body he had had in his youth, still had somewhere under that enormous paunch, the same square shoulders and a face with Indonesian features that grew less distinct with each generation. We were beautiful – well, perhaps not beautiful as such, not gemlike, but striking, people noticed us. "Feral," said someone. "Solitary," said someone else. "Glorious," said the man who took care of us. "Cheap little cookies," said our mothers in our dreams. So much was said, and most of it you have to ignore, but we were restless and hungry, we were starving, we took everything in. In our own creation story we had been born out of each other's heads, emerging from a dream or a thought in one of the others. We dreamed of each other when we fell asleep on the shore, we dreamed of our mothers. We often ran away, but we always came back; we had nowhere to go.

Our clothes were faded by the sun to a shade of old rose and faint apricot, worn thin by time and salt water, and over the years they grew softer and softer, until the material was sheer as silk or skin. Enormous insects lived in our wardrobe, crawling around in the fabrics, grasshoppers and dragonflies drawn to the dark and the damp. A dead bird had made its grave in one of the shoes and there we left it, and afterwards its blue and white down clung to our petticoats and jackets. We took the wardrobe with us when we moved to a new place, and the piano, which travelled in a cart at the back. We moved frequently, always heading somewhere, never seeming to arrive. It was old and heavy, that wardrobe, with clothes spewing out of it like a little volcanic eruption.

It had been a long time since we had known which clothes belonged to whom, maybe they had never been owned by any particular one of us. It didn't matter: if a dress was too big, we took it in with safety pins, and it didn't bother us if it was too small, we liked them to be close-fitting and feel tight. Our guardian wasn't wealthy, but nor was he poor, and he had a flair for getting people to open their homes to us. Money was therefore seldom a problem, yet still a poverty of a different kind beset us. No rituals, no rules, no plan for the future, no photograph albums or any other evidence of our existence. A man and three grubby kids who were always on their way to somewhere else. Like gravediggers we lived in the hereafter, life always just out of reach, as if we had already missed it or would pass it by at any moment. Each time we decamped we threw everything into brown trunks, the dead bird as well, preserved by time, like in a museum, cold and pure with a hint of mothballs. We travelled from coast to coast, the grey and white sky streaming along above us was all we knew. The place where our wardrobe stayed longest was the cottage by the lighthouse, which could only be reached when the tide was out. We had imagined that we were never going to leave that place, and in a manner of speaking that came true, at least for one of us.

The lighthouse cottage lay at the point where the earth ended and the ocean began, and beyond it there was nothing, as far as we knew. It stood on an island that became a promontory when the tide retreated, and living there was an old lady to whom we were distantly related. Further along the shore was a quarry, and the mist that came off the sea in the mornings enfolded our world in a gentle light. Our relative was ancient, so old she had the air of someone from another species. A first we thought we were just visiting, as we usually were in other people's homes, but after a while we realised we had moved in. On some days it was so still at the lighthouse the air began to quiver, the sun's rays met the earth, and the sky seemed to rise into space. The water lay like a mirror to eternity, and if we hung over the edge of our little boat with our goggles we could see hundreds of metres down into the smooth ocean. We hadn't even unpacked, we walked around all day long collecting seashells and watching the tide rise and fall. The shells were small and delicate as a girl's pudendum and you couldn't hear the sea inside them properly, not even on quiet days when our own ocean wasn't clamouring at us, but we could hear voices within, speaking wisdom, prophecies, mystifying riddles. It had been so long since these shells had harboured life, so long since they were emptied, cleansed by thousands of years of ocean water, but the voices had remained. One day children of the future would be walking there and would hear us calling from the shells. Too late then for intervening in our life.

The days passed and we didn't leave. We got used to the garden without noticing and we had started calling the old lady Nanny or Mamie. In the afternoons we sat on her bed and weighed her smooth, heavy skin in our hands as if it were gold. The skin hung loose on her body and was worn and diaphanous as a silkworm chrysalis, and so soft to touch it made us yearn to be old and more sheltered. The hair on her scalp was thin and tufty, often concealed beneath a sky-blue nightcap. We were waiting for her to die, that was why we were there, but it was slow, death wasn't particularly interested in a woman so old and insignificant. Perhaps it thought she had been taken long before. It wasn't only the man we lived with who had fallen in love with this place, we had too. We ran beside the thundering ocean, we built dens and made swings and bows and arrows that we suspended from ropes in the forest, without a thought that we were really too old for things like that. We would go for a shit out of the den windows and when the swings flung us right up into the sky, we would take a pee. We watched the huge ships come from nowhere and glide over the horizon's rim. Not one of us could swim when we first arrived at the lighthouse cottage. We walked into the water in our clothes, cautiously dousing our feet and ankles, but never further than that, and when the waves reared up at us, we raced back to the beach.

There were just the three of us in the world, the rest were shadows, including the man who looked after us, like the bats that flew past us when we went out at night. And all the time we explored each other. Tracing a finger along the crook of an arm or over a knee. When we lay outstretched on the sand with the sun blazing down, our complexion turned golden and our hair grew darker, and every day new signs appeared: a scratch, a cut, marks left by night-flies and dragonflies, a snakebite, a faint sprinkling of freckles, moles that one day were suddenly there on our thin skin, like a splatter of paint flicked from a brush. Sores, bruises, dirt, grey streaks.

"Maybe one of us is Christ."

"Or is going to die young."

"Maybe we all have a life somewhere else."

We slept next to each other, we woke next to each other, we always watched each other, and yet we missed the crucial thing. The shore by the lighthouse was like a vast mirror meeting other mirrors, capturing light from the skies and the waves in grains of sand that glinted with millions of water prisms, and all of these formed myriad sand reflections in which the clouds mirrored themselves.

"Time to come in now," and we ran in the direction of the lady's frail, tremulous voice in the twilight.

We had never been interested in swimming, but we learned fast, like dogs. We knew that the tides would pay us little regard. We had taken a swimming manual from the lady's library and we lay on the sand in our dresses, practising. It was easier than we could ever have imagined. First we learned how to swim long distances under water and soon we could hold our heads above the surface without drowning. We were used to home-schooling, used to learning things by ourselves. The sea was always cold, drawing ice streams from the north. Inside us our mothers came and went like wraiths, appearing in our dreams, the only place we met them now.

"Come on out, little baby cakes," they called, and we raced towards the voices. In the dream they were always a single dark silhouette without a face.

"Here we are," we shouted in the last wisps of dream, before we were dragged up into the light and our narrow beds. The shouts from the night lingered, a residue of sugar and cool rain. Hanging inside our clothes were lockets bearing photographs of our mothers. We compared them with each other: one chestnut brown, one pale grey and the third a redhead, like an orange. All day long we would lie and look at them, the silver cases moving at our throats where a little frog pulsed under the skin, marking time. We were laden with ticking clocks and graveyard soil, our mothers had gone off with the master plan and it felt as though they had taken the entire firmament, or at least the bright, high heavens of long ago, and left us with an upended sky, grey as innards, blurry, half suspended. But we took what we were given, we never hoped for more than what was before our eyes.

We used to watch the tide ebb early in the morning, laying bare everything that had been concealed on the wrinkly grey seabed: starfish and shells and bladderwrack and billions of tiny translucent crabs crawling in the light, just as surprised every time. The water loitering on the sand after the waves withdrew formed large pools for the clouds to drown in. When the sea swelled again we rowed about in a broken-down motorboat and just before the blue hour we rushed out to run in the unbridled sunshine. Those evenings when we were waiting for something to happen, it seemed as though it was the last light we would ever see. For every correct answer in our home-schooling we were given a sugar candy. Our pockets were full.

"Tell me something that lasts forever," said the man who was our teacher, our protector, our companion.

"Time!"

But did any of us know what time actually was? It wasn't exactly a piece of candy you could hold in your hand and gobble up or save in the fold of a dress to annoy someone else.

"Watch out!" said the man who provided our care, and

he threw a glass onto the stone floor. And we learned that time was the difference between the whole glass and the glittering shards lying in front of us. Had there been no time, the glass would still have been whole.

We shot up, protesting.

"But what if nothing happens? Like for us here, where everything stands still?"

There was no candy that day.

And time passed nonetheless. Inside the body. It was slowly decomposing, desiccating like a prune.

The days at the lighthouse were identical and yet full of life. Lanterns in the trees swayed in the wind, music floated out of the house, an ant crawled up a leg and disappeared under the hem of a dress. There were shiny green bottles all over the garden, mostly empty but harbouring a wondrous aroma, and small bowls of sour apples and black apricots. We were always ravenous with a hunger that had nothing to do with the stomach, but it helped to fill it, and we ate to survive, to grow heavier, to prevent the dreams taking over. There were dangerous dreams, villainous dreams, dreams featuring criminals in which you might even be a gangster yourself. And you could always blame a dream if you wound up taking your own life.

*

Our overcoats and jackets were full of gaping holes, they were moth-eaten and ugly, but it didn't matter to us. The linings were pink and sagged, making it look as though they were bleeding, like animals draining on meat hooks. We didn't want anything new. The old lady was continually picking through her dusty clothes to find something for us, but we didn't want it. "You are what you are," we said, wriggling into our old coats. We had seen our mothers' eyes gleaming in the sand among the shells and seaweed, and we would lie on our stomachs at the water's edge with our legs in the sea and keep watch over them. They had left our world, but for a time their gaze had remained in the sand.

When we felt like taking a look around, we walked out to the road to get a ride somewhere. Cars seldom passed so it was an event when they did. We lay in the middle of the road waiting, looking up at what was going on in the sky. Some days it sped past faster than the cars, but on others it was absolutely still, and then it was like being caught in a vice of nature, everything motionless, unending, irreversible. The sound of screeching brakes always roused us from the torpor that engulfed us, but none of us died. We were screamed at by strangers instead of getting a lift. No-one wanted to pick us up: we were too stupid, too reckless, we might have absconded from an institution that would come after us if they drove us somewhere. That was what they said, then slammed the doors and roared away. Crestfallen, we trudged back along the road, into the forest and on towards the sea. We always hurried home to catch the tide. The man was waiting for us. On those occasions we were late, we had to swim across. We placed our clothes and our watches and shoes in a little bundle on the top of our heads and then swam over to the lighthouse in the half-light. We were still children of a kind, still hidden by corn plants and reeds wherever we went.

We dreamed a great deal. That was what there was to do. We lived as much in our dreams as outside them. There were the lucid dreams, the ones where we realised we were dreaming and we could take full advantage by doing whatever we liked, illegal things, forbidden things: we mastered the skills. Rape, robbery, theft, fights. We threw ourselves on pretty women and kissed them, we haggled with sleaze-bags. We were always shouting to each other in there so we wouldn't get lost. When we realised it was a dream we responded by charging at the walls to escape the narrow world in which our lives were enacted. There was one window we avoided for ages that was open, banging in the wind, the window that looked out towards death. We drank perfume mixed with Coca-Cola and it gave us the urge to be off again in the hope of a ride somewhere, but before the tide had started to turn and we could still have made our way over to the mainland, we were already drowsy and apathetic. The exhilaration perfume induces is ethereal and tenuous, and it isn't just that you exude a fragrance, but that it feels like flying machines lifting off, and you forget how to live without the intoxication. You are left lying somewhere, filled with an erratic flickering light. But somehow in the dreams we always got away. We sought out the nearest town, to which we always got a lift and where we drove without a licence. There we met men who tore holes in our coats and ripped our dresses, who found their way into our underclothes as though there were treasure inside. We flew over snow-capped landscapes. When we were awake we promised one another we wouldn't jump from a height in our dreams, but then later we could never resist. We threw ourselves from precipices into ravines. The giddiness as we fell to the ground was heavenly, the feeling of invincibility as our heads struck the rocks but didn't smash. In our dreams we had wings, we could feel them moving on our shoulder blades as we slept, their old mechanisms creaking. Grey and white and huge, they smelled cold and muted. When we awoke the wing odour lingered in the room. We rested in each other's arms, exhausted, until we fell asleep again.

*

One of us couldn't read and the other two read very little, mostly the Bible, but at least we knew how to follow the black letters that floated like a fine tendril of pinned insects, rousing the shadows around us, giving life to them. It wasn't like that for her: the words got tangled up, she became distracted, glassy-eyed, tossed the book aside. Not that we had many books, we weren't able to have much in the way of things at all, but the few we had were prized possessions, and the lady had a large library. We could devote entire days to standing there reading the spines and as we traced our fingers over them whole galaxies would open up. We adored the Bible, the thin shiny silk pages smoother than human skin. But with time the Bible acquired a little water damage and the pages became spotted and stiff. We took turns laying our cheek against the red book, and nailed a cross up above the head of our beds so that nothing should happen to us. There were some other things that separated us, apart from our mothers: not being the same age, not being the same height, and our feet not looking the same in the sand. The one of us who would leave first was also the one who had come into the world last. She had a special glow about her, the light in our life until she became our great darkness.

And so it was that our sister died. She lay dead in her bed. On a Sunday. There were pale striations all over her body that looked like teeth- and claw-marks, as if she had fought with bears and angels. The lady was still alive, like a stubborn old clock. A little monkey sat on the piano stool and was playing when we came down that morning to the large room facing the ocean. As soon as it caught sight of us it ran to the window, clambered out and vanished into the early mist. If it hadn't left dirty marks on the ivory keys we would have believed it too belonged to a dream. For a long time we sat staring out over the sea. We woke our guardian.

Our sister was still lying in her bed. If we looked at her for too long we imagined she was still breathing, a feather still moving inside her. But her small person was encased in flesh and blood and it was this flesh and blood that now would moulder to dust. Everything looked distorted and soiled, including us. We carried her down to the beach. From a distance it looked as though she was sleeping with her sunglasses on, but up close her pallor stood out, an ash-grey colour, and she was no longer sunburnt like before. Our keeper, who now had only the two of us to care for plus a little corpse, dragged our old piano down to the water's edge to play funeral music under the open sky. Perhaps he hoped the music would transport him away on the winds. In music you were innocent, he said, in music there was no world, no rules, no restrictions, no disasters. We who were left laid our heads on the shiny black wood and wept, and the piano thumped like a heart. Our weeping echoed inside it, but was mostly drowned out by the roar of the sea. The saltwater left white streaks in the piano's gloss when the waves splashed over it and retreated, just as it did on our chests when we emerged from the sea, and in the end the beach would swallow half the piano, which sank slowly into the sand. But first there was this, the notes rising out of its black body and skipping over the shore like gusts of wind or sand fleas. From a distance it looked like a giant black insect had landed in the middle of the beach.

We buried our sister in the garden under the Indonesian tree. We couldn't keep her; she was so changed after she died. The first morning she still had a shine in her eyes – we saw it glimmering under her eyelids as she lay in her nightgown – but now it had gone, and the features on her face were heavier, almost washed away, as if she were a sculpture that was nearly complete, but not quite, a work of art that would never be ready, and none of us was Michelangelo or Jesus.

We sang a little homemade song and we thought she would come walking down the beach when we had finished, but of course she didn't. We lay flat on our sister's grave and sang other songs and tried to speak to her. She was annoyed down there, so she didn't answer. We heard her swearing under the ground. We poured sweet cherry juice onto the grass, the kind she liked. Or had she stopped liking that? Was she someone different now she was dead? Someone we didn't know? Had she forgotten us? We couldn't picture ourselves without her, but she turned away from us in her grave.

"Don't be angry with us," we called.

She didn't reply, but we stayed there, hoping she would hear us, and most of all forgive us. Her voice was stronger than ever down there, and for the whole day we lay straining our ears to listen. It was like someone talking in their sleep: you could hear the words but the order they came in made no sense. We never played the piano on the shore ourselves, but from time to time we sat on it and gazed out over the sea, watching the silent ships appear out of the fog on the horizon, seeing the waves being hurled towards land and then receding. Foggy days were still the best, when a downy light enveloped everything; the worst days were when it was so clear we thought we could see into the future. We buried the lady after she had finally been gathered into heaven, or somewhere.

Weeks passed, months too, and perhaps years. Most things were the same as before, apart from the fact that we were two instead of three. We walked up and down in the sea, we stretched out on the sand and basked in the sun, we swam and collected things that had fallen out of the sky. There was a new century, a new millennium to boot, people said, the third since the birth of Jesus Christ, and that night we stood on the beach beneath an exploding ether and wondered what would become of us now. We thought we might have loved one another too much; we thought we might not have loved one another enough. The doors to our wardrobe blew open that night and huge waves crashed into our room. Suddenly it was full of water, shimmering green and crystal clear. We were swirling around with chamber pots and old sanitary towels, ribbons and bows and musical boxes. Nothing felt the same after that, and neither did we. We discovered that we had grown up without noticing, that now we were sad young women without dreams. The two of us who were left waited for the tide one last time and then waded over to the mainland.

Life after the lighthouse was simpler and emptier, more vaporous. Our weight went down and so too our expectations: hope weighs more than you think. We were thin husks of the people we had once been, and yet we began to live a different kind of life, a life more appropriate for women of our age and station. We went through a series of medical examinations which determined we were no longer young, we were already getting on. We started working in an office, we got married, we gave birth on a narrow delivery bed. You could say that we had plenty of happy days, even though there was always something lacking, like an old entrail left behind in the road dust. We were no longer pretty or fat, nor special or particularly foolish, and it was a long time since anyone had called us cheap little cookies. And as far as we knew, the man who had looked after us for a whole lifetime was still at the lighthouse, playing the piano, with the little monkey at his side. We would dig his grave one day and deal with his effects.

AMERICAN HOTEL

When we met, Vladimir took photographs of elderly ladies who lunched. No-one was interested in his photography, but he persisted in badgering various galleries in east Detroit. Everywhere in his small attic apartment hung pictures of women alone on exclusive restaurant terraces, looking vulnerable and out of place amid the skyscrapers, like precious lost dogs, but at the same time having something monumental, immortal about them.

"That's what happens when we're dead," he said, grabbing me and kissing me on the neck under my hair as I walked around in his studio that first time. "We're transformed into stills of ourselves. It happens in the blink of an eye."

"I know."

"How do you know?"

"I was writing a dissertation about it. But I've packed it in now."

"Pity."

"No, it's fine. It got too difficult. Or I was just sad."

"Did the dissertation make you sad?"

"I think so. And my mother died. Though I definitely don't want to talk about that."

Vladimir liked my long hair even though it was matted and dry as straw, the little braids, the flowers and glass beads I used to wear then. He liked the blonde streaks that quickly turned to silver. He called me Carter, Nixon, Reagan, the Wurlitzer Building. That was at the beginning. Later it was just Carter. *Don't leave me, Carter. Kill me, Carter.* I moved in with him the very first night. I had on my white jeans and my DaimlerChrysler sweatshirt.

Sylvia always said that death would come early. She saw all the wars that would follow. She said it's love that tears a person apart. She said two towers would burn far away, that people would fall from the sky like ash, that America's revenge would be sevenfold, the great wars that resulted in distant places would cause vast swathes of people to start migrating across the planet. She lived so briefly and she knew everything as she lay dying in her porch swing under a grubby shawl. I sat by her bed in the hospital for weeks, writing, while she drifted in and out of her coma.

"I keep thinking I've missed a room at the American Hotel. One room out of three hundred. I've forgotten to lay out new soaps and towels."

"You haven't."

"But it feels like it."

"The hotel isn't there anymore, Mom."

"Isn't it?"

"It's in ruins, like the rest of the city."

"Well, there you are."

She didn't look as though she believed me.

"Besides, you're the best cleaner in Detroit. You'd never miss a room."

"Yes, cleaning I can do. I deserve a fricking prize."

She looked at me with her intense gaze and raised her slender, scrawny arms above her head.

"Say it all so you don't regret it later. Tell me the worst. That's what you're supposed to do in this kind of situation. I'm ready."

"But I have nothing to say. You can bring your hands down."

She lowered her hands to the blanket, but she was smiling, perhaps her last smile.

"I'd expected more deathbed histrionics. A bit more accusation and reconciliation and drama."

"I'm just so glad you existed."

*

I sat next to her on a folding chair, writing my dissertation. My dissertation was to be on the subject of the skeleton in classical drama, the skeleton as a representation of the evil within us, the shape of the ghost and the wolf we always carry inside us, but guard ourselves from when we see them in real life, at the doctor's or at a museum. I thought that the skeleton was also an outline of man, a hastily drawn matchstick figure or the beginnings of a portrait, and that deep inside we belonged to the same scrap of raw humanity. When Sylvia fell ill I abandoned that plan, and as her skeleton became more and more clearly visible under her taut, pallid skin, I drifted to new topics. Crime in August Strindberg, birds in Anton Chekhov, O'Neill's nights. I did it for her sake, though she had no notion of what it was all about, just as I had competed for her sake, had run the sixty and the one hundred metres since I was a child. Sylvia was undaunted in the face of death, but I saw it grab at her like a hand, and I saw the shadows gathering around her bed. That was the summer I met Vladimir and Jack. Death was clutching at Sylvia, and I was clutching at life.

The first time I met Jack, Vladimir and I had only been seeing each other for a few weeks. Jack was rich and quick as a snake and lived in Indian Village. Always expensive clothes, jeans and sneakers that had cost a fortune. He sat and stared at me on their parents' old sofa on Kingston Road, as I knocked back drink after drink. There was nothing that suggested the two of them were twins or even distant relatives.

"Well. Where did you find him?"

"On the telephone," I replied.

"On the telephone?"

"Yes, I was selling stuff. Car insurance."

"Vladimir's never had any money to buy insurance with."

That was what we did in those days. Everybody worked in automobiles in one way or another, everybody loved autos. One summer I was making calls selling insurance; we started talking and couldn't stop. He was on his own, I hated my job. The easiest people to sell to were the old and the lonely, their voices thin and full of hope. That summer, I would fantasise about my father answering on the other side of the continent and recognising my voice. Jack looked at me in a way that suggested he was making a quick calculation in his head.

"So you have had a job?"

"Hasn't everybody?"

"Not everybody. If people had made a little bit more of an effort, the world wouldn't be in the state it's in now."

I thought of Sylvia. She really had made an effort, she

had done her utmost, and still it hadn't been enough. She worked double shifts so that I could carry on studying, she took the bus at dawn and returned home at midnight, and everything still went down the tubes.

"And what do you do now?" he asked.

"I compete," I said. "I run."

I knew he was wealthy, that he had earned a colossal amount of money in a short time. He was a photographer too, but a successful one; he had photographed people who had died destitute, who had no family. It had changed him. "Jack gives off the whiff of money now," Vladimir had whispered as we got out of the car. I thought it was mostly the whiff of loneliness.

"Tell me what you want," he said.

"More whisky, I'd like to have another drop of whisky." I held out my glass, empty again.

"How much?" he said.

"How much do I drink? I never drink when I'm competing."

Jack filled my glass to the brim with the shiny amber liquid.

"Tell me how much you want or you can leave by that door."

Vladimir was suddenly standing in the doorway before either of us had heard him.

"Are you coming?" he asked, and disappeared again.

On the way home Vladimir was silent and I waited for him to say something. The city sped past, its empty streets, carelessly parked vehicles with smashed windscreens. After a while I asked:

"What was all that about?"

"He always does that with my girlfriends."

"I don't even know if I understand what he did. Don't you get angry?"

"Anger was many moons ago."

He flashed his quick smile. A bird dived out of the sky and plunged into one of the abandoned cars. I envied birds their precision, their instinct for survival.

Sylvia slept her sleep of death under the shawl and I wrote my dissertation. Later, when she had gone, I couldn't bear to continue with anything I had been doing before. I stopped running and I stopped writing; I had needed someone to do it for. It was so empty after Sylvia; I was an adult, but I felt like an orphaned child. Something in her death changed me. I never recovered and things started to collapse around us, it wasn't just me. Everything that had been there when I was a child was suddenly gone: people, gardens, life in the streets. Sometimes it felt as though my childhood had just been a dream.

*

The last time she woke from her coma, her hand knocked over a glass of juice onto my notes and she began to speak about my father. She had never spoken about him before; maybe she had thought the grave was the best place for secrets. Anyway, she had changed her mind now.

"What was he like?" I asked, as I fingered a photo of the man with silver hair and dazzling blue eyes whom I had met at the Lee Plaza a long time ago. There was something girlish about his thick lips and his smile.

"Your father is a Christian con man, but you might need him. Find him, he's the only one who can help you now."

"How will I find him again?"

"You're sharp. You'll find him."

"What about you?"

"The worst thing about dying is that now everything's going to pot, I won't get to see it."

"You do know I'm going to miss you very much?"

"Don't. When the world ends I'll come back to you."

There was something that made me go back to Jack. The very next day I found a reason to return to Kingston Road and I stood there ringing the bell. Jack didn't look especially surprised, neither pleased nor displeased, when he saw it was me. He simply opened the door, backed into the darkness and gave me the cardigan I had left there the previous evening.

"You left this."

"I know."

"People leave things in places they want to return to."

"I often forget things. It doesn't mean I want to move in."

Then I made a tour of the house, examining all the objects, and he followed me like a shadow. It was the old parental home and most of the things looked the way they must have done when they moved in sometime in the '60s. Light and airy wooden furniture, heavy brown curtains, a lot of glass. Their parents had moved to Molokai in Hawaii and they seldom heard from them, a single wedding photo on the piano. Pictures of him and Vladimir on the driveway up to the beautiful white house. He said Obama came from there and Konishiki Yasokichi, a sumo wrestler I had never heard of.

"Won't they ever come back?"

"It's not that strange for someone to want to leave this city. Have you never longed to disappear? Of course you have."

"I've never wanted to disappear. I hate it when people do."

In hindsight I think I was sleepwalking that autumn. Was it because they were twins that I allowed myself to break all the rules? Because there was already something ghostly about the situation, a defect, a doubling-up, a mistake of nature that could excuse me? One soul in two bodies. Or was it because everything else in the world was on a path to destruction? I remember the rosary that was dangling from his hand as he showed me around. I stayed for an hour or so every time. We didn't sleep together, that wasn't why I went. This was something else. We lay on the rug in the living room, playing chess. We played for money, not large sums, but I always won. Jack was too rich to have any competitive spirit.

I continued visiting Jack. As soon as I woke in the morning I grew restless and wanted to go. We didn't have a particularly good time, and yet I still had a desire to be there. The interminable chess games when I had to wait forever for him to decide on his next move. As if each move were as significant as the choice of a new partner or the purchase of a new car. The stifled light behind the curtains, the food we ordered, the booze. After a while, of course, we started to sleep together. I don't know why. Perhaps it would just have been too odd not to have done. Sex was the only thing that could explain such irrational behaviour, visiting that desolate house. I didn't like going to bed with him, and he didn't like going to bed with me. It was cold and impersonal and weird. Even so, I got pregnant straightaway.

"I'll just tell him straight," I said. "Vladimir will understand."

"You have a high opinion of him."

"Yes, he's my friend."

"May I ask one thing?" He stared at me, his eyes blazing black.

"If I can leave after that."

"Why don't you move in here?"

"Great."

"I'm serious. Why don't you?"

"You're joking."

"I'm not joking. I never joke. You know that."

"And Vladimir," I said. "What are we going to do about Vladimir?"

He laughed and took hold of my hair, twisting it round his wrist and pulling me towards him.

"Yes, what are we going to do about Vladimir?" We gazed at each other.

"We don't even like one another," I said.

"You and Vladimir?"

"You and me. Vladimir and I like each other very much."

So I went home and told him it was over. We lived in an attic room with a skylight, the rent was almost nothing, and we shared a toilet in the corridor with a Persian family and a single woman from Shanghai. I lay on the floor with my hands over my face. I didn't dare to look at him. I thought he was going to hit me, but he was just silent. He kissed me between the legs on top of my white jeans and asked me to leave. It was as if he had known from the beginning how it would end.

I don't believe that Jack ever liked me very much. I was a thing between him and Vladimir. He loved Storm from the first moment. At the hospital he lifted her from my breast before she had time to start sucking. I thought that was so beautiful, that there was something appealing about being a daddy's girl. Jack renovated the house and removed the old '60s curtains. He sat for days in front of Storm's doll's house, papering the tiny rooms. He bought a canary for her. It was as if her existence in his life roused him from a long sleep. He could play with her for hours, his patience infinite, unlike mine; I was impatient, nervous, inadequate, too scared of losing her to see her properly. And Jack despised frightened people.

"I'm just so terrified someone will take her," I sobbed.

"But we're the only ones who want her. She's a minute, overweight, self-centred little creature who vomits all over us whenever she has the chance and who wakes you in the middle of the night because she fancies something to eat. What if I woke you up every other hour and asked you to get up and make me a sandwich?"

"But I love it when she wakes me up at night. I lie and look at her, her tiny dark eyes like little lamps."

As soon as I closed my eyes everything fell apart. I saw it clearly before me as if it were a film. Behind the image that was us flickered another image. One that was more real. Where we went without food and were freezing. Where Storm was hungry and I had nothing to give her.

Vladimir loved Storm too. Everyone who meets her loves her. She has a special light around her, a presence that makes people feel chosen. The first time Vladimir saw her, he forgave me. He couldn't tear his eyes away from her as she lay sleeping in a basket on the floor. But what do I know? Perhaps there was never anything to forgive. When he lost our old rented room, he started coming over; he came in the morning after Jack had gone to the office and stayed all day, watching TV and helping me with Storm.

"I never thought you'd be a mom."

"Me neither."

"But you are."

"When I'm out, people look at me as though I'm the Virgin Mary. As if I'm a good person just because I'm dragging a kid along. Everyone smiles at me. They never did before."

"Sounds nice."

"It is nice. But unexpected. As if I'm no longer suspicious. Do you want a hold?"

"No way. I'd definitely lose her."

"You wouldn't."

"Yes, I would."

"That doesn't actually happen. As long as you're not in the habit of leaving your heart behind or forgetting one of your legs somewhere."

"It would happen to me," Vladimir said.

"But you wouldn't leave me behind anywhere," I said.

"Maybe that's the problem. That I can't forget you."

I couldn't forget either. I waited for it to pass, but it didn't.

"Everything's a mess out there. Honestly, it's all turning to shit now," Vladimir said, when there was nothing left to say. "It's like coming to a different world here with you. It's like it's always been."

"What about you?"

"I've got a whole skyscraper to myself on West Grand Avenue. The whole effing Lee Plaza."

"Really?"

"Not really. But I've got half the sixteenth floor. Like living in the middle of the sky. And I think there's a meaning to all of this."

A meaning, Jack said, is for idiots who don't have

anything to hope for, who can't accept the laws of nature. He said what was happening now was raw nature. When I had Storm I thought she needed to have a mother who was good at something. A mother who counted. After she came into the world I thought more and more about my father. He inhabited the fringes of my dreams, rushed past in a winter coat and vanished as soon as I turned. And immediately before I fell asleep at night, his small, crooked smile came to me. How was it possible to think so much about a person you had only met three times? The first time with Sylvia at a railway station, where we hastily shook hands and he looked as though he was in a hurry to leave. The second time at the Lee Plaza open-air café, where I sat with a huge glass of Pepsi in front of me. He smelled of eau-de-Cologne and interrogated me about my plans for the future and my relationship with God.

"We should live our lives as if Jesus is coming back this afternoon," he said, looking up at the sky with his brilliant blue eyes. That was at a time when there still was a future, when there still were gods. I was thirteen years old and I had learned from Sylvia that fathers weren't for us.

One day Sylvia had taken time off from the hotel and spent it all in the stands at the arena, flicking through a magazine. Now and then she looked up and her eye sought me out on the track. I have never run as fast as I did that day. I ran until the sun went down and it was dark when I laid my head in her lap and wept with exhaustion. On other occasions after training I would go and see her at work. I used to sit on the bed in one of the enormous rooms at the American Hotel with a view over the entire city and watch as she transformed piles of soiled sheets and towels into yards of clean, smooth linen. There was something unreal about those rooms when we left them, as if we had cleaned up the evidence after a crime. All the rooms were identical, and the air-conditioning and the automatic lighting created the sensation that it was one single, asexual, artificial season inside there.

Everyone else apart from Vladimir changed their plans when the world changed around us. People turned out to have incredible ingenuity. They grew accustomed to living on nothing; it was rumoured that they started eating the stray dogs that were prowling around in the city. Not Vladimir – if he couldn't photograph women eating lunch alone amid the skyscrapers, he didn't want to do anything at all. He started to take an interest in gravity, in people who deliberately fell out of buildings and trees. He talked about discovering a supreme truth that could only be found in the laws of nature. He started saying that we should leave the city, and that I should take Storm with me. A thought had lodged inside me like a knife: *What does it matter that my child is thriving, if all the other children perish?*

"What kind of world is this for Storm to live in," said Vladimir in the empty skyscraper at his end of town. "Take Storm and come back to me."

"I can't take her," I said.

"Well stay then," said Jack in his garden where the sprinklers were constantly whirling round and the lawn mowers kept chewing at the burned-up grass. "Stay with me and Storm."

"She'll be better off without me," I said.

"Where did you get that idea from?"

"I don't know. It just feels that way."

"She needs you more than anything else. You do see that, don't you?"

"No, I just don't get it."

"I've never met anyone who knows as much as you do, and then you don't get this."

I wished he would hold on to me, but he didn't. Later came the white nights, when they set fire to everything and I had left Storm. Devil's Nights, they called them. The stench of burning hanging over the city for days. We walked around in the ash, Vladimir and I, and it was just us again. It had really always been just us, and I remember thinking that at least there was something that was greater than missing Storm, a loss that seemed to be affecting the whole world.

*

When I moved into the skyscraper there were seabirds everywhere. We scared them off later on. Vladimir was always lying over by the window, in the same position whether I was coming in or going out. In the afternoons I sat in the old Olympia arena, spectating. Close up they were like beasts of prey, the runners. I loved that tremendous power, it was almost brutal; they had a perfection I wanted to be near. When I came home Vladimir nagged me about helping him die.

"Come on then, Carter. When are you going to do it?"

He could so easily have done it himself, thrown himself out of the broken window on the storey above, but he wanted me to help him. *It has to be you, Carter.* Personally I thought taking your own life was something you did yourself.

"If I beg you?" he asked.

"You've begged me a thousand times."

In the fierce sunlight by the window, Vladimir was playing with his gun. He looked at me with a gaze so intense I was forced to turn away. I felt naked and sober, although I had been drinking for hours. I didn't get drunk anymore; the more I drank, the clearer everything became.

"How can you ask me such a thing? I hate you having that pistol. I'm always scared."

"Are you scared of me?"

"A little."

"But it's not you I want to hurt. I would never do that."

"But aren't you still a murderer if you want to kill someone, even if that person's yourself?"

I touched his thick arm. It was warm and damp and pale, both hot and cold at once, living skin. The freckles, glowing, were so profuse on his upper arms, they joined up. We were never in the sun anymore, but perhaps he had a dark sun inside him that continued to shine.

"I'll always love you," I said, and lay down on the floor. Vladimir let the whole of his weight sink down on top of me; it felt as though he was already dead, but maybe it was because he had grown so fat. He looked exhausted in the harsh green light. He must have been as tired of these conversations as I was; we could have recited each other's lines by now. I missed him already. I missed the people we had been before.

In the last vestiges of sleep I was reaching out for Storm, for the shape of her little bottom, for her chubby legs and the nightdress that rode up slightly on her back, her breathing as light as a feather. When I woke up, a cold silvery light was falling across the floor. Vladimir was sitting by the window, an unlit cigarette in his hand.

"When I'm gone, you can go back to Kingston Road."

"Wouldn't that make you sad? Or jealous?"

"I'll be dead," he said, lighting the cigarette and taking a few quick draws before stubbing it out on the rug.

The electricity came back temporarily, making the fluorescent light on the ceiling buzz and flicker like a thunderstorm. A faint light filtered through the tiny gap between the doors of the elevator.

"When are you going to do it, Carter?"

"Sometimes I wonder if that was the only reason you wanted me to come back, so I could help you die."

"Why did you really come back, Carter?"

"You know why. Because I like the person I become when I'm with you."

"And who's that?"

A silver aircraft flew past at low altitude. A military jet. For a moment the roar filled the entire building, before it continued over the city. I didn't want to tell him I became nobody when I was with him. That was what I loved.

"It has to be you who does it," he said finally, when I didn't reply, "otherwise it would feel as though I was abandoning you."

*

I could sit in the Olympia arena watching endlessly; when the runners passed by close to me I breathed in the smell of adrenalin and blood and potential. The emphatic propulsion, like a river beside me, like this city long ago. There was often just one slip of a white guy training. He was small and tireless, ran for hours at an even, unhurried pace; it was hypnotic. Each time he passed me he caught my eye and I smiled encouragingly, like a parent to a child. On one occasion he came up and asked for my number. If I'd had a telephone I would have given it to him, if I'd had the strength I would have asked him for his. I could have done with a friend, I could have done with a friend who was still running. Life had become so bare, like a skeleton robbed of its flesh.

I always thought I would go back to Storm, when she turned five, and six, and then seven, but I didn't. Then I thought I would let her be, that was the only thing I had to give her, but there I was again, in a telephone kiosk a long way outside the city, dialling Jack's number. Her small voice was suddenly right beside me; I imagined I could stretch out my hand and touch her. She was only a few miles away and yet it felt as though she were on another planet or in another century.

"Hi, Mommy." She sounded so tiny on the telephone, like a cartoon character.

"Hi, Storm."

"Hi, Mommy," she said again.

"What are you doing?"

"Nothing."

On the other side of the pane of glass a radiant sun beamed out of a clear sky.

"What do you do when you're doing nothing?" I said, closing my eyes against the sun. She was quiet for a long while, just the sound of her rapid breathing in the receiver.

"Play."

Then:

"Were you scared of your poppa when you were little?"

I suddenly realised it had been a long time since I had thought about the man with brilliant blue eyes. You believe you are always going to have something in your mind, and all at once it has subsided, like a stone inside you.

"Well, I only met him a few times, so I didn't really know who he was. But he was ever so strict, I think. I probably was a bit frightened."

"What were you scared of?"

I thought about it.

"I don't really know. That he didn't like me, maybe."

"Didn't he?"

"I don't think so. Not much, anyway."

I think the very last time I saw him he was sitting alone on a bench in Grand Circus Park. Storm was only a few months old and was lying awake in her pram when I caught sight of him as he sat reading a Bible. He looked old and his clothes were black with dirt. He appeared to have aged several thousand years since the day I sat before him at the Lee Plaza. On the path in front of him, he had placed a paper cup for passers-by to throw money into. *Live as if Jesus is coming back this afternoon*, it said on a small sign beside it. When I went up to him to say hello, he asked me if I could help him with a few coins; his voice was shaking, his eyes had lost their blueness and were clouded by a milky white film, and nothing in his face indicated any recognition.

I paused for a moment, with Storm's shallow breathing in my ear.

"Are you scared of your poppa, Storm?"

She was silent for a few seconds. I could hear the sound of the sprinkler in the background. I knew how everything looked: the grass, the tall trees, the light, the fireflies, his hand on her shoulder.

"Never. But I was scared of you sometimes when you lived here. When you were with me and you were drinking."

And then I did it. I shot my beloved. I thought I didn't know how to use a gun, but I did. I started shooting and I couldn't stop. It felt as though I was killing myself, the roar inside me, the devastation, the blood that was howling and screaming. And Vladimir was still alive, he wasn't dead, he was weeping as only the living can weep.

"I've changed my mind, Carter. I don't want to die."

"What do you mean?"

"I don't want to die," he wept. "I just wanted something to end. But I don't want to die like this. You have to ring someone . . ."

"But my dearest one, there's no-one to ring."

"Ring Jack."

Storm was sitting in the back seat, looking at me through the window. I took her by the hand and we ran up the 1,422 steps behind Jack. At first I thought that Vlad had gone, as he wasn't by the window, but he was lying huddled up against the wall next to the elevator. As if he tried to come out, to crawl after me, a bloody trail running all the way to the elevator. He looked as though he was sleeping peacefully in the sunlight, but when I touched his wrist it was still.

*

A slender ray of moonlight was suspended deep down in the sky. The skyscraper swayed slightly in the wind, as if the world were tipping; I felt the movement of the tectonic plates beneath us and the distant pulse of the Atlantic waves pulled by the silvery moon, the reptiles forever frozen into the rock below us. Storm had fallen asleep on my knee, her hairline damp with sweat. Only occasional neon lights flashed in the darkness.

"I could say it was me," Jack said next to me, in a voice I had never heard him use with anyone other than Storm.

"Why would you do such a thing, Jack?"

"I'll say it was jealousy. It's quite logical. It might even be true."

I wanted to laugh. The world in which jealousy existed felt infinitely far away, like a mirage.

*

Sometimes Storm and I are woken by an albatross flying along the corridor outside.

"Look, Momma," she shouts. "Look Momma, a seabird."

She runs after it until it disappears through a broken window further down the corridor. The seabirds fly to the great grey lakes. Lake Saint Clair and Lake Erie. Over the Detroit River to the Atlantic. In the big cities in five hundred

years' time, all traces of us will have been swept away,
birds of prey will have occupied the airports and auto-
mobile plants and deer will stroll around alone on Michigan
Avenue.

THE SEAHORSE

I thought Ray was unemployed, like all the others. He would spend all day at the Seahorse drinking Blue Oceans, and I thought, I bet he doesn't have anyone waiting for him at home either. When it turned out later that he had been sitting there on my account, I was astonished. He was in love, he said, he'd never met anyone like me, and he was going to leave his family. At first I didn't understand any of it — *in love, haven't slept for weeks, police officer, married with four kids, going to give it all up for you* — we had hardly spoken to one another. Once or twice I had been standing in the bar waiting for another order and he had asked me something, about the Seahorse, and maybe I had occasionally lit his cigarette. It didn't matter what had happened; a policeman who looked like a villain was irresistible.

"But I'm just a regular swine, Rebecca, not a devil, if that's what you were hoping for."

Sitting opposite me on a bar stool he looked as though there was a landslide inside him, a precipice, a mountain ridge.

"So what have you done?"

"I've done the best I could."

He had nothing big on his conscience. A bit of drink-driving, some krokodil he had forgotten to hand in at the police station, a few under-age girls, a sick, neglected wife. Nothing two or three Hail Marys wouldn't help.

I had been sacked from my job at the shop in Tangoio for advising the few customers they had against buying any of their ugly wares. Handbags and wallets in alligator and lizard skin. If they asked, I told them straight that no-one should have to pay for such a hideous bag, and I gave stuff away a few times to people who didn't have enough money, those who insisted on buying something anyway. The owner was a guy with a toupee who was seldom there. He must have thought that the image of me would draw them in, but my presence had the opposite effect, the customers hated me, eyed me askance behind my back as I stood demonstrating wallets. They were mostly tourists, folk just passing through; no-one from here could afford things like that, and it wouldn't even occur to any of them that they might ever need such things. At the Seahorse I let everyone pay, everyone knew what they wanted and everything was worth the money. Alcohol is purer than belongings and banknotes. You know what you're getting: the immense wave of heat flowing through your blood, its value timeless as a gemstone. Do, who came night after night, was the only one who didn't need to pay. I never had the heart to take her money, although she was doubtless on benefits like all the rest. She used to arrive in her tracksuit bottoms and a skimpy T-shirt with a fluorescent print, she had watery blue eyes and fluffy grey hair, and she always sat at the back of the bar and smiled broadly at everyone who came in. She sometimes wore a quilted jacket even when it was warm outside. When she held out her small, well-thumbed notes, I would ignore them and wait for her to push them back into her purse. Often a little circle of stillness formed around her and if she neared a party of people, they would fall silent until she backed off. But the smile on her face never faded, however many times she was rebuffed, and as soon as anyone looked at her, she beamed. Sometimes, after I had finished my shift in the bar, I sat and talked to her for a while. She was often my last customer. As a child she had been a beauty queen, and I wasn't surprised – I had known all along there was something splendid about her. She still moved as if beneath her shabby appearance she was someone special. Occasionally she showed me photos of the person she had been and it made me think that ageing for beautiful people is crueller; it is a shock to see how time has stripped their faces.

Strangers were drawn to our house next to the power station, first with the hope of Violet becoming theirs and later with the forbidden thought it was going to be me, the sullen daughter. When she withdrew to her bedroom or fell asleep in the hammock, they started prowling around the house in search of more wine or something to eat. And then they would think of me. Every now and then they would wake me during the night and sit on my bed and tell me about their lives, always slightly drunk and amorous and as if they were close to something, an abyss or a little flame. It was only to me they told the truth, talked about their weaknesses, their crimes, their irreversible mistakes, their tragedies. Once one of them stole my booze while I was asleep. In the morning, when the light had gone from their blood, they sat grey and helpless at the kitchen table, waiting for Violet. Some days she had already left for work, and the house was silent and sad without her. It sometimes felt as though Violet was younger than me; she was slapdash and childish and possessed a strength and a concentration that I have never had, a playfulness and a sweet gaucheness, lighting up every room she entered. And the strange thing wasn't the attraction these men felt towards me, it was the change that took place within me, how at first I was scared by their presence and habit of swarming around me, only to gradually swivel in their direction, and how I started to wait for them, hope they would turn up again and present me with gifts and compliments without me having to do anything.

Since I had started working at the Seahorse, everything was different. I had my own money and the nights were filled with voices and faces. When the sun rose I cycled home along the coast. Violet and the Vulture were both sleeping on sunbeds on the veranda. I was the only one who called him the Vulture, and he hated it, but he was abnormally tall and thin and always walked with a slight stoop and seemed to float through our house like a giant bird suffering from depression. He was constantly sucking on his pipe and hitting his head on our light fittings, which according to him were hanging far too low, but it wasn't the light fittings that were the problem. Nonetheless, my spiteful little soul made the Vulture tender-eyed and hopeful and he spent hours just trailing behind me to talk about my life. His overtures included bathing suits and curling tongs, comic books, badminton, darts, ladybirds, butterflies. It gave him an advantage because no-one else retained their interest in me for any length of time.

Violet didn't like me meeting Ray. She didn't like the police or anyone to do with the authorities. We had never accepted help from anyone, even when we might have needed it. Violet had tried to school me herself all the way through and although it had been rather sporadic, by some miracle I passed the yearly tests. But sometimes I think I must have missed something fundamental, something that might have helped me get away from here earlier. So I didn't tell her much about Ray, let him drop me off at the beach and then walked the last bit home. Often I lay down in the hammock and slept away the remains of the night there.

I had come into the world when Violet was sixteen. She had been so young, all but a child herself, and had given birth to me here at home on the kitchen floor. I had slipped out of her like a little octopus and she had washed me herself in the sink, laid me in the bed next to her and pushed a bottle of milk at me. Sometimes Grandmother had come round with some tinned food and newspapers and a little money. But then she turned out to be some kind of evil Witch and stopped coming. All there had really been after that was the two of us, until the skulking spectre of the hunched Vulture had shown up. In a way we had grown up together, Violet and I, and I soon caught up with her; at twelve I was already taller than her and by sixteen I was taller by a head. I never knew whether my love for her was reciprocated. We were more like siblings, or puppies.

Violet was often cantankerous and moody. She would sit on the veranda, smoking, wrapped in a blanket, dressed only in vest and pants, her legs drawn up under her, her face closed, turned away. Long ago I had been frightened of that face and the shadows that abruptly passed over it like a solar eclipse. Now I knew she would be back in an hour or so. They had nothing to do with me, those shadows; it was the Witch moving across her face.

"Where have you been?"

"At work."

She didn't think the Seahorse was a job for me, but that was because she had no concept of who I was. I had nothing inside me of what she had hoped for. And the Seahorse was like me: a silent night, no more, no less. There I learned everything I needed to know about the world, about loneliness, about love and poverty. Ray had found me there. Can you imagine?

I thought Ray was like someone out of an old-world fairy tale. He told me he loved me even before we had slept together. To me, saying something like that was unheard-of.

How could he know? I had never known anything like it.

"You might not even like the way I smell," I said.

"I like everything about you," he said, "and I've smelled you every night in the bar, that's why I sit there, to breathe you in."

Oddly, I couldn't recall any of the evenings, or I couldn't tell them apart, there had been so many; and when I was mixing drinks and filling bowls with peanuts and greasy crisps, there was nothing else. The people sitting in the bar drinking were the same to me as what was on the shelves: bottles of booze standing in rows, waiting, night after night, all having the same effect and the same appearance, always the same story, and both the bottles and the customers created the same sense that this very moment was all that existed. I lived my life fast at this point, like a candle flame, or at least that was what Ray said. He said he took things slower.

"That's not true," I said, "you're the one who wants to leave your whole life behind and your sick Ruth, even though you don't know anything about me."

"Not true," he said, "I've spoken to you every night at the Seahorse, I've told you all about my life, I don't need to meet you one more time to know."

Ray would appear in the afternoon at the bar counter looking gloomy. He had that way of looking down into his beer and then looking up again to stare at me, searching like an old lighthouse, imploring. I actually hated those Rimbaud eyes. After a while, there it was again, the same flash of terror. He dragged his love for me around like a scourge.

"But listen, Officer," I said, holding his gaze as it swivelled between me and his beer, "are you always this dramatic? How on earth have you managed up to now?"

"But I'm not! I'm known for keeping my calm, dammit!"

"Sure, Ray," I said, secretly pleased to have thrown his life off course. "Don't you know that everything passes?"

He pointed to the golden owl on my chest. I had owned that top for so long, the print had almost vanished.

"Not this."

"Okay."

The darkness always disappeared in the end, he ought to have known that, and the light did too. How could he have lived so long and yet know so little?

"My life has just fallen apart," he bellowed, as if he were Hamlet.

"I don't believe that."

"You're too young to understand these things."

"I'm not that young, in actual fact. On paper I'm as much an adult as you are."

He fiddled with his gun and pulled a dog-eared book out of his pocket. *The Lagoon*. He had brought it with him the last few times we had met. He had read ten books in his life, he said; he was the only one around here who read apart from Violet and me. Do gave a discreet wave from her table and I waved back. I didn't want her to have to wait.

"What's your book about, Officer?" I said.

"It's about you."

"Weird. I'm going to serve Do now."

The intention was that we should do home-schooling regularly, but it was always quietly forgotten. Some days we sat on the veranda aimlessly leafing through my new books on geography and mathematics before abandoning them in one of the many piles of newspapers or stacks of books. I read everything I could find in our own house and elsewhere, I didn't need the books from school. Maths I learned from playing chess, love I learned about in tattered magazines. Once in summer and once in winter people came from Hastings to inspect us. We sat at the kitchen table drinking coffee and answering questions that had nothing to do with school.

"Where's her dad?"

"God knows," Violet said.

Well, you could only hope that he knew, at least.

"I'm going to work at the power station," I said.

"And what about school?"

This was when the atmosphere would always change, the cheery tone giving way to something glummer and putting us all on our guard. In front of our little audience we made a haphazard hunt without success for the books they had given us last time they came, but that didn't matter, there were always shiny new books on the history of mankind and linguistics and the English language waiting in the postbox a few weeks later. As for my father, I had never asked about him. Some questions shouldn't be asked; either there are no answers, or you can't live with those there are.

On my twentieth birthday we celebrated in the garden, Violet and the Vulture and I. They stayed up all night and kept on partying, while I lay on a blanket on the grass, drifting in and out of sleep and watching their shadows in the light from the lanterns in the trees. Her small head, her long black hair, the smoke slowly rising from his pipe.

"What are you going to do with your life?" Violet asked, her face suddenly close to mine as I surfaced from a half-dream with her lying next to me on the grass.

"Nothing," I said.

They laughed, she and the Vulture, and I sank back into

the quiet land of sleep. In my dream the Vulture's shit was in boxes and tins all over our house.

Ray came to the Seahorse every night. He flung open the door as if he was royalty, and maybe he was, with his cop's badge and gun and uniform. He glanced around, searching for me, and when he saw me behind the bar counter his face brightened, and I wanted to have that sun that was inside him, the sun I could elicit and that I would one day extinguish.

"A bourbon . . . And I'd like you as well, if I may . . ."

"I'm yours whenever you want."

"Are you really?"

"Yes, but maybe we shouldn't talk about it all the time?"

"Who have you loved most?" he sometimes asked, presumably thinking about my previous boyfriends. About Quentin perhaps, about his sad eyes behind the bar in the Seahorse, his broken teeth, his square face, his five o'clock shadow that appeared only a few hours after he had shaved.

"Violet," I said.

"Yeah, but Violet . . . mothers don't count."

"After her there's no-one."

"What about your dad?"

I thought about it for a moment.

"I guess you don't love ghosts either."

"And what about me?"

"What about you, Ray?"

"Do you love me?"

I told him straight, that I loved him, but that I would destroy him.

One day I went to Ray's house. It was larger than all the others, unbelievably big, almost ridiculous, and there was a dirty pool at the back. I didn't knock; I wasn't a guest, I was something else. I came to take care of what Ray didn't deal with himself. The atmosphere in the house was airless, sluggish, a faint smell of ulcers and unwashed genitals, as if it had been a long time since anyone was here, even though Ray and the children must have been there a few hours earlier. The huge kitchen was a mess, cups and half-eaten sandwiches everywhere, an empty wine bottle beside a single glass. In the living room I discovered Ray's drinks cabinet and poured a glass of whisky, which I took upstairs with me. There were plush carpets in all the rooms, making the house strangely quiet. The curtains were closed everywhere on the first floor, but music was streaming from a radio in one of the rooms and I was met by a dim glow when I opened the door. Ruth lay asleep next to an open window, curled up like a child, her long grey hair across her face. Apricots and pastilles were scattered on the sheet next to her. Medicine bottles and discarded water glasses were squeezed onto the small bedside table. A light breeze blew through the room as I sat and waited for her to wake up. When she woke she looked at me intently, but without concern, without surprise. Her eyes were large and bright.

"Are you from the council?"

"Yes."

"Did Ray send you?"

"I'm just supposed to be here with you," I said, "but we have to keep it as our secret. Can you manage that?"

She nodded. I asked her what she usually did all day. She stared out at the mute white sky.

"Nothing. Sleep a bit. Death's never going to come, is it? Nor Ray."

I didn't ask about her illness, it was probably the only thing people wanted to talk to her about. I offered to massage her back and I rubbed her with a thick, granular ointment, and then I fetched whisky and sandwiches from the kitchen for us both. It didn't seem to matter to her who I was, whether I was death or a last angel.

I cycled there for a while every afternoon before work.

"Do you only come to me?" she sometimes asked.

"Of course I do."

When she fell asleep, I would also drop off for a few

moments on the floor or at the foot of the bed. We played cards and read aloud from her school Bible. She had started reading the Bible now, somewhat at the eleventh hour: "I can't face reading anything else," she said. Not because she was religious, but because the stories were so pure, so naked, because it all went belly-up for everyone. Just as it had for her. Every time I was about to leave, she held my hand tightly, and I thought that underneath her dreadful illness she was beautiful as an elf, as a tree. It was difficult for me to imagine that Ray slept here with her at night after he had left me. On the bureau was a wedding photograph in which they were so young they were almost unrecognisable; an absolute innocence pervaded the picture, and the young versions of Ray and Ruth stared at me while I lay in their bed.

After a while I no longer knew who I liked better out of her and Ray. I plaited her hair, I washed her, I made her laugh though it hurt her fraying lungs.

But the whole world revolved around a bum hole, two hungry balls and an insignificant little bush. I didn't believe in love, but I did believe in this: Ray holding my arms in a vice over my head in the dunny when only Do and a few others were left in the bar, muttering to themselves half asleep in their seats. And late at night Quentin coming by and cashing up, and the notes he gave me always coming to a smaller sum than the tips I had received during the evening. The longer the night went on, the more money the customers left on the counter for me. Quentin threw some of the sleepers out as he did his rounds like a bull on the prowl. As soon as he had gone I would turn up the music and offer Do another glass. When Ray stood in front of me in the bar again, he was a stranger. There was nothing in him I recognised and his hangdog look made me defiant. I would close the bar, we drove Do back and I walked the last bit home along the shore.

I loved watching Ray while he slept, because then he was someone else, someone who couldn't defend himself. I loved observing him when he couldn't see me, when I could feast my eyes on his face. He was so vulnerable lying there asleep in one of Violet's shirts, in her bed, while she was at work.

"I can sense that everything's going to fall apart," he said when he awoke and reached for me.

"Why would it all fall apart?"

"Because I'm old and you're young. Because you have everything ahead of you and most of it is already behind me."

"But I'm lying here in front of you," I said, stretching out on the bed, small, coy and foolish as I was in those days.

"I don't want you to find out how old I am," Ray said.

"How old are you then?"

I had forgotten to ask.

"Forty-eight."

"That's no age for a horse," I said, and climbed on top of his luckless body. "Anyway, you've got to go now, Fatso. Violet will be back soon."

"Don't you want to smoke a last cigarette with me?"

I reached for the green cigarette case, tapped one out, lit it for both of us and then lay back on Violet's enormous pillow and looked at him.

"Have you killed anyone?"

"Why do you ask?"

"It's one of those things that's good to know. About someone you love."

He laughed and without finishing the cigarette he stubbed it out in the ashtray I was offering.

"That's true. No, I've never killed anyone."

"Yet."

One afternoon in the house with the pool we were in Ruth's bed dozing in the bright ocean light, me behind her back with my arm around her, when she whispered:

"Don't you want to meet my husband, Ray?"

It was pouring outside and the rain smelled good, making the whole world out there pure and true.

"I'm not keen on policemen," I said.

"But maybe you'd like Ray."

"Possibly, but my family has had a few issues with the police."

"Ray isn't bothered about things like that, you'd realise if you met him."

"I don't want to meet him."

She persisted.

"Sweet little thing, I'm quite sure you could do this for me. After all, soon I'll just be an old corpse."

It was still raining when I cycled away, and it continued to rain for weeks. The small roads around town were filled with water, a stinking grey deluge, and everything floated away in it: flowers, bodies of tiny animals – ferrets, rats, birds – and my pens and books that I had left on the veranda. Our dresses and underclothes and the Vulture's shirts on the washing line were carried off by the rain. I never went back to see Ruth. I blamed the rain, and for a few days the Seahorse was closed as well, because the rain had come in and it had flooded. Violet and the Vulture and I would spend entire days sitting on the veranda watching the sky release everything it had, a curtain of warm water between us and the rest of the world. When the rain finally stopped, Ray filed for divorce, took the children and left Ruth on her own in the house. A few months later she died by her ocean window, where she and I had spent so many afternoons together. By then I had already ditched Ray and left my job at the Seahorse. By then I had left town.

I remember that the lizards used to glitter like gold in the headlights of Ray's car when I came out of the Seahorse late at night. Do was standing a short distance away, smoking a cigarette in the silvery liquid light.

"Do you want a lift anywhere?" I shouted, waving at her.

"If it isn't any trouble for you pure young souls."

"He's not that young," I said, and opened the door for her.

Do came with us all the way along the coast road, sitting quietly in the back, half asleep, her head against the window. Drinking as she did was exhausting. Her house was where the sea ended and the pine forest began. She climbed out and gave a slight bow before she walked up towards her dark little abode. When we reversed back out into the road, we saw her in the headlights, squatting to have a pee. We drove back along the coast and saw the first glint of the sun on the sea and the first clouds rolling in over the horizon, before Ray dropped me off outside our house. Those clouds came from so far away, lit from within, their life so brief. The tops of the pine trees looked as though they were on fire in the dawn, and I saw clearly as if through a magnifying glass how they were all grabbing at me, Ray and Quentin and the Vulture and Violet's many night-time friends. But I was young and fast, so fast I could still run away from them all. And I ran, without knowing where I was heading, and when I finally arrived many years had passed and all of them had grown old and lost their lustre. When I see them now they are somehow frozen, fixed, and yet still there, illuminated inside me, all the people who appeared and disappeared in our life, Violet's and mine, during those final months in the small town next to the power station. And despite the fact that I know what happens to them — Ray will drive into a cliff one August night a year after Ruth's death, the Vulture will vanish without a trace, as silently as he entered our life, and Do, she drowned below the Seahorse a few years after I had left, Quentin will continue to tend that bar like a baby — inside me they are still radiant and enigmatic. Violet is still sulking in her hammock under the lanterns with the Witch, who came back when I left. It has been a long time now since I heard from her. I still love her. I always will.

THE FAMILY

They flew to Agadir. She rested her head on his shoulder in the airport; she was tired, she was scared of flying and she was longing for a cigarette. You weren't allowed to smoke on planes anymore, perhaps that had been the case for a long time. He was tapping his foot, a rather fidgety foot that was always on its way somewhere else. Whenever they were walking in town she would end up a few paces behind him; he was always in a hurry to get on with life. It was a last-minute trip, the kind of thing you could find in the newspaper in those days. They had made their minds up there and then. She fell asleep on the plane before the in-flight trolley came out, sleeping in the cosmic light with the grey wig pulled down over her eyes while he drank a Campari with a parasol. When she awoke they were somewhere over the Mediterranean. The plane lurched and turned in a westerly direction, away from Europe.

Agadir was angular and sun-bleached and looked slightly makeshift, with a reddish dust coating everything. The heart of the city was the many new tower blocks – youngsters in the world of skyscrapers, but skyscrapers nevertheless – between which the pair wandered around. The buildings looked like oversized teeth. Mangy camels trudged along with their keepers on the beach below their hotel. Their matted coats hung in tufts as they floated out of the quivering haze, weary mirages of silver. Boys who were still kids and old men with sun-dried faces, their arms covered in cheap wristwatches, zigzagged between pale, languorous sea lions wallowing on sunbeds, gorging on sun, sugar and booze. The two of them walked around without knowing what they were in search of, as tourists do the world over, waiting to be gratified by the buzz and beauty of the planet. It was cold, a damp, creeping chill coming in from the sea. She had a jacket over her dress and bought a shawl to wrap around her; he wore a white linen suit, never felt the cold, his skin made smooth by the salt breeze and the North African light. They lay on their backs beneath the sky and the clouds that endlessly drifted away, she with the wig over her face.

"Do you have to have that on all the time?"

"Yes," she said, twisting it so that the grey hair fell into her eyes.

Her brother had worn that grey wig towards the end – it still had his smell. She wore it everywhere as a last salute to him, not really knowing who she was now that he was gone. His death had been caused by an accident so silly it looked as though it could have been self-inflicted, but her brother hadn't been silly, far from it. In the afternoons she stood at the hotel reception desk with a telephone receiver in her hand. She had forgotten how heavy old-style telephones were, and the dial was so slow, as if she were in a nightmare. She had a funeral to arrange back home, a funeral so difficult to organise she was afraid her brother would go without.

They took the bus to Marrakesh and found a small window-less hotel room where there were cockroaches crawling along the walls, and at night, when she couldn't sleep, she watched their progress. They took the bus back to Agadir and the dazzling sea and she lay awake in the moonlight while he slept his gentle sleep. He could always sleep, and when dawn broke and the muezzins sang out their calls she sat on the balcony with her legs drawn up under his shirt, looking out over the silent, motionless ocean, waiting for him to wake. When he did, he came out into the light with narrow eyes, then he went to buy bread and coffee and dates and brought back flowers for their little balcony table.

There they sat and witnessed the city begin to stir. Every now and then they closed the door facing the Atlantic to rest from the light for a while. She wore the wig when they made love, a choice he accepted without a word. He bought her books in Arabic and summer dresses and a little gold tea service. She had no money with her; he was the one who had paid for the trip and he was paying for everything now they were here too, which made her slightly submissive and extra hungry. She jotted things down in a brown notebook when he wasn't looking. They had an understanding that she wouldn't make notes on the trip, but she never kept her promises. She had a feeling he was in a relationship with her shadow and that he made do with that. She was never really a match for that shadow. He said he was happy with her, that he would never find anyone else like her, but obviously he would, if she did leave. He was cut out for life, so to speak.

On their last day in Agadir a black kitten floated ashore. She saw it in the water and every time a wave broke, it rolled further up the glistening sand and was then sucked back down with the foam and tumbled around before being washed back up onto the sand again. She picked it up and laid it in the wig where she let it dry. Its eyes were closed and it had salt residue in its thin fur. He said it could be full of disease and that she shouldn't touch it. She pressed her mouth to the cold little nose before she walked up to the reeds to bury it, wrapping it in her T-shirt when he wasn't looking. When they packed their cases, she sneaked the little corpse in under everything else. They made the same journey back across the sky, through a world of industrial grey on the airport bus, like one of the many sea-green postcards perpetually bound for the homeland as proof that its citizens had been out in the world. They entered her small apartment with their suitcases, the scents of sun and sand already gone from their clothes. An envelope was waiting for her under the letterbox, with no postage stamp or frank, but bearing a gold seal, and because it was pale blue and had no postmarks it looked as though it had fallen from heaven. But be that as it may, it was a summons, something regarding an assignment in another part of town. The sender was a secret society for some elderly gentlemen and a few ladies, all of them on the same steep slope towards death, whose function was to collect and catalogue a number of objects seen as cultural. The letter was rather battered, as though it had been held at the post office for some time. It was like receiving a message from another age. It was signed "Your devoted brothers", which indicated the matter was already settled, the period of consideration was over. She slept on his chest that night, the night that was to be their last together, though neither of them really grasped why, just that this was how things would be from now. He said he would always love her and the next morning he left before it was light. When she awoke he had already been swallowed up by the city.

She signed an agreement to be faithful to the Society for life, to belong to no societies other than this one. She moved her belongings from the apartment she had inherited from her grandmother and into an apartment in the city's most beautiful district, where the streets were wide like boulevards. She received some items of furniture and a special allowance to buy a dress slightly more appropriate for the wild parties that would ensue. She chose a black dress that resembled one of her old ones, though it cost ten times as much, and sent the bill to the gentlemen and the few ladies. She donned the new frock, put on the grey wig and a full-length cloak and was picked up by a black hackney cab. Inside in the cab's half-light a cocktail was waiting for her and a chauffeur who looked so much like an anteater that, during her many subsequent drives with him, she would convince herself he had stepped out of a dream. She stood outside her new address with two suitcases that looked rather worn and handed-down – made of cracked white leather with a silk lining – and looked up at the dark windows. She leaned her head against the facade and breathed in the smell of other times, of piss and screams and soot. A weak autumn sun touched her face, and in a way it was autumn in her life too. She had a vague feeling that she had somehow misread life and it was too late now to correct the misunderstanding.

A sleepy janitor opened the door when she rang the bell, bowed slightly and showed her up to the dark but spacious apartment. It was high up, the steps were crooked and winding like a staircase in a funfair, and the top of an ash tree pressed against the windows. She hated trees. Folds of heavy velvet curtains hung by the windows, the rooms were dark and unnerving, the wallpaper had scratch marks which would be taken care of, the janitor said with a blank expression; that would never happen. As she wandered through the tattered rooms that were now hers, it looked as though someone had tried to find a way out through the walls. The wide street outside led to a square where a chestnut tree grew, obscuring the little light there was, its roots forcing their way up through the asphalt like fossilised reptiles. On the first few evenings she ate alone in a small French canteen next door, ordering mussels and absinthe. Having brought a book about the Atlantic to read, she surreptitiously flicked through a women's magazine under the table. When she was going to sleep at night in the ragged room, she could see the oak trees by the entrance to the harbour from above, as if she were a bird flying over the downy treetops that curved like a green ocean beneath her. On the ground under one of the trees lay her brother's dead body, the raptors tearing at his sailor's shirt to reach the entrails. One night when he was drunk he had climbed a tree in the harbour, fallen to the ground and broken his back. Now he would always be the young man who had fallen out of an oak tree. Now he would always be in the hands of gravity, that old seducer.

The first meeting was held in a castle inspired by the Winter Palace in Saint Petersburg, situated on a hill that sloped down towards the water below the Cathedral and close to the Supreme Court, the National Library, the Remand Centre and the City Hospital Archive. The archive was implanted in a rock as though in a catacomb, and people said that patients still roamed around inside, each bearing their nameless cross. A few years earlier she had sat there herself, reading her paternal grandmother's journal on behalf of a family association and seeing her grandmother's character shine through in the journals, seeing her unwavering soul pour out in the cold hospital language. She hadn't known then that this was where the most illustrious Society was located. Now she walked up the steps to the palace where she would stay until the end of time, a palace guarded by soldiers with bayonets, young boys' faces hewn in stone. The bayonets turned aside, one by one, as she climbed the stairs. You were cleft by a sword when you made your entrance, or you were admitted: either way something was cut off forever. The bayonets made her think of Archimedes and arithmetic, that if this castle constituted a firm spot in the world, then perhaps from this one spot she would be able to move something outside herself. She forgot that a body immersed in water loses not only its own weight but also its significance. The displacement of water says nothing about people's weight or importance in places such as this, and, what's more, being here was like eternally wading along under water, immense, cold and glittering green.

The first evening there was an emperor at her table, the empire having had links with the Society since the beginning of time. Her country no longer had gods, but an emperor was a different matter. The actual emperor next to her was tense and slightly gauche under the mellow champagne bubbles; he squirmed and grunted and muttered while the empress and their imperial children moved effortlessly between the halls with a ready smile for anyone who hungered for one. She felt instant fondness for her table companion, sensed his isolation in the room, and since the emperor was a chain-smoker, so was everyone else on this first evening, with a wad of cigarettes standing in a glass on every table. When the emperor reached for something to smoke, so did everyone else, everyone except her, who sat squarely on her chair like a stubborn child and refused to smoke. She had been given instructions that he wished to be addressed as Emperor, to which she had no objection; she had come across people before who wanted to be called all manner of things. For a short period as a student she had sold sex and had learned the art of being called anything at all without ever divulging her real name, and to call them whatever they wished: Daddy, Jesus Christ. This emperor wanted to talk about cars and parenting, not her strongest subjects — she didn't have a driving licence, for example — but it was easy to follow his tangle of thoughts, choleric and wide-open as he was. That very morning he had shot a female boar in the face, he told her. Her lips formed a little "Oh", and then an "Ah".

She was welcomed into the Society, like a grandchild coming to visit during the holidays, like the future embodied. Her new colleagues offered her sweets and grapes, they sang and they talked, they took one another by the arm and strolled through the many halls. They gave her a place that would be hers until her death, for everyone in the Society had their own little throne on which to rest their posteriors. Hers was gilt with fussy details and the padding was greyish yellow and flattened by all the behinds that had reposed upon it in the past. Her predecessor on the throne – who now operated in the Society from his grave in the manner of a ghost – had argued his way through his last decades in the Society, left and returned and left again like a boomerang, and in addition to the constant disputes, had devoted his entire life to homosexual sex in the works of Marcel Proust. He was alone in this, since there was no-one in the country apart from him who had read further than page 26 in the famous suite and reached the eroticism, but perhaps the others had been deterred by the Normandy waves pounding incessantly between the pages.

As far as work was concerned, it was just a matter of pitching in: there was a lot to be done. She stuck at it, sorting, cataloguing, her table laden with venerable objects. During working sessions they gathered at a table in the Hall of Mirrors, which was between the Hall of Strife and the Hall of Beauty. It was in reality slightly too large for them and certain of the gentlemen appeared to be drowning in their thrones. At one window stood a small bronze head depicting a deceased member of the Society who had made himself known for being able to write in mud. She always felt as though she was being watched by the stern little head. In the room a huge carpet lay rolled out, with motifs from *One Thousand and One Nights*, a book she had adored as a child. The carpet's design made her feel safe and at home. Worn smooth by all the feet that had tiptoed around on it, it shone in the dim grey light filtering in through the windows.

She had her place in the Hall of Mirrors next to a gentleman who in time would become very dear to her. He was rather grumpy and drank cognac for breakfast, lunch and dinner and snored his way through all the major decisions, but sometimes he came to and gave a little soliloquy. She hoped that he would live forever, that the chair next to her would never be empty. He had the same air of laid-back impudence and elegance about him that her own family had once had, her father, aunt and grandmother. Sometimes during protracted sessions this gentleman – well, for a gentleman he was quite rough-and-ready, but this was how they spoke in the Society – would push a note across to her. As the little piece of paper was unfolded he would chuckle behind his hand. His two penn'orth on dramas short and long that unfolded around them, battles small and large, digressions and fallacies. The gentleman's bits of paper made the time pass – it would obviously pass with or without these notes, in the same way death comes with or without our wish – but all the same, on the long evenings they were rabbit holes. The gentleman's father was miraculously still alive, even though he might quite reasonably have been dead, and he sometimes accompanied his elderly son to the Society. It was an endearing sight, the two old gentlemen coming along the boulevard, grumbling, arm in arm, and the younger of them being dropped off at the door by his father with a kiss on his broad forehead.

It was like returning home after a long journey. Her new family was like the family she had once had; they were lofty and rather apart and they breezed along slightly above reality, in a soap-bubble world. The rules of this Society concerned the ceremonies first and foremost, the glasses, the walking pace, the singing. In other respects it was more like the Wild West. Perhaps her first family's loftiness had been mostly in her father's somewhat sinister mind. As a child she had believed they were world-famous, which they were not. They were more like outcasts, but that had its own advantages, allowing her always to move between worlds seamlessly, like a faun. Now she was the only one left in the ashes of this fantasy. Her brother had been the last one in her first family to depart. Their mother had been dead for decades, having slipped out of their lives with minimal fuss following a short illness, and now it was as though she had never existed. In his old age her father had been revealed as a fraudster and a crook, and following that revelation the two of them had lost contact. Now he sat alone in front of the television, wondering where his life had gone and waiting to see her face appear on the screen, which it sometimes did, like a princess from a foreign realm. The crowning glory of his wretched life's work was to cheat her brother out of money. Her brother, who was a gentle, defenceless soul and had never been capable of saying no to their father, had been persuaded to take out grotesque loans and invest the inheritance left to him by their grandmother in lifeless, non-existent businesses. Her father's second wife was also dead. Perhaps she had opened too many doors in his gloomy old castle, but in any case she was lying by his first wife's side in the family grave, waiting for him. Their magnificent grandmother had sailed into death the previous year, no big deal. It was just time sweeping over their family. Now, when they were all gone and there was little left to hope for, this unexpected and quite bizarre piece of good fortune had befallen her.

One day she was given time off for her brother's body to be viewed at the mortuary. She had to organise several different viewings, because his old boyfriends and lovers would have murdered each other if there had been a crowd of them next to the body. Four times she received a party of tearful men and boys outside the funeral parlour, four times she heard their wails inside the room.

No-one in their fold could remember precisely why they were elevated, but they knew that they were. It was something to do with their lineage or some other distinction they had been awarded back at the beginning of time. Some of them could remember nothing at all, they simply sat with childlike, happy, shining faces, fingering their medals. Behind these shining faces, it was said, were old rulers, but she was too young to remember great powers and great battles. All she knew was that for some of them it was hard to find their bearings, but that there were people who could help. One day they would help her too, one day they would take care of her few possessions and dig her grave. It truly was a homecoming.

Some evenings it was like visiting her grandmother again in the asylum where the patients sat with their fake medals and proclaimed themselves to be Christ and Napoleon and Marie Antoinette. Even the ceremonial acts were reminiscent of the rituals of sickness, with the mania and the trust in dreamlike details, the fear of persecution.

It had been difficult to get to grips with and had taken some time, but she buried her brother. She didn't want him to be alone under the ground. It was a small, inauspicious event. In the mortuary on the morning before the funeral she had dressed him in his sailor's shirt and laid a Billie Holiday gramophone record beside him and whispered things he couldn't hear into his ear.

"What were you doing up in the tree? You didn't think you could trick me, did you?"

His delicate features were already merging into something heavier. That was the way death worked, erasing everything you loved, coarsening it until just mould remained, and now he looked as though he had been drawn in great haste by a careless god. Their father wasn't present at the funeral. He was weak and infirm as old men who have lived hard often are, and he was in hospital and couldn't travel. Perhaps he had made himself ill to avoid being there. It was just as well; her brother's friends would probably have thrown stones at him if he had shown up in church beside the coffin. It made it simpler for her as well. She was tired of Jesus and Nietzsche always having the last word on forgiveness. Even if she did forgive her father one day, there would still be no forgiveness.

Time rolled slowly on. The mood in the flock was generally one of languor, somnolence and calm, but sometimes a spark flew through the Hall of Mirrors and someone stormed into battle. On those occasions, the usual mild-mannered atmosphere proved to be a thin veneer covering a brutal power struggle, but that was the case in all relationships involving people; it wasn't peculiar to this association. She believed that they, like all humans, had within them the potential for full-scale war. She liked all the members of her new family, in the same way that she had adored her first family with a fool's love. They all had their merits. They also all had their weaknesses, among them vanity and a particular kind of unwittingness and the facile institutionalisation that is a common result of this sort of arrangement. Sometimes during long meetings she removed the wig and placed it on the table in front of her. Her own hair underneath was wild and black, and what was growing out now was coarse as bristle, as though she were related to the witches who had avoided the stake. When she sat on her oversized yellow throne and contemplated the splendid bronze head by the window, she was seized by a special, wonderful self-forgetfulness. The head turned unhurriedly in the grey light, sometimes with its gaze fixed on her, sometimes on one or other of the gentlemen, before closing its eyes and taking a short rest in death.

"What do you think about forgiveness, little noggin?" she asked.

The head didn't like questions and it stopped moving.

She settled down quickly in her new life, getting used to the fat-laden fare at ceremonial dinners and to receiving letters from culture-loving gentlemen who happened to be visiting the city and wanted to meet her. Many an evening she walked across the thousand-year-old pattern on the carpet in her shiny high heels that were slightly too big. The Society bore the cost of the high heels too.

Hanging in the Blue Hall were huge oil paintings of both gentlemen and ladies, captured at the height of their achievements. The paintings were redone every year, since most of the gentlemen and ladies were dissatisfied and repeatedly wanted something improved. The first few times she had been in there, for various preliminaries – when she signed her name in an enormous book, when she practised dancing in preparation for the ceremonies – the artist himself was present, sitting in a corner, sketching the old portraits. The portrait painter was fussy and rather deferential, bowing and scraping to everyone he saw, but beneath the obsequious surface he was angry as a hive of bees. He painted jerkily and slightly too fast, taking a gamble, pulling it off more often than not, and of course he had aeons of time, for those portraits would never be truly finished during the slow transformation of their occupants. He wasn't necessarily the most eminent of his calling, but several members of the Society were impressed by his way of skimming over the realities somewhat, especially since they themselves were almost manic sticklers for etiquette. Perhaps he should have been replaced long ago, but now it was too late; he was an indispensable part of the furniture, a dear old mutt no-one had the heart to shoot, a bossy tub-thumper marching around among them with an old walking pole and a baton and a broken mace. If she stared at the portraits long enough, she could imagine them living inside their paintings, a remarkable double exposure on those evenings when they were swarming around in the halls beside her. The ocean at Agadir still stirred within her, its blinding light still blazing behind her eyes.

When she walked around looking at the portraits, she heard whispers coming out of them. The gentlemen and the few ladies were calling out, buried under the many layers of dark oil that formed a sombre, foam-whipped sea. She could stand for hours gazing into the world of the paintings, trapped as they were in a row, slipping imperceptibly out of time. In the centre was the portrait that over the years had become suspiciously similar to Picasso's painting of Gertrude Stein. The painting had been redone many times throughout the decades the subject had spent there, and many versions of him lay within it, layer upon layer of a learned man's memoirs. She would have liked to get to know all these layers, in the same way she wished that each version of her brother still existed. As her brother had grown up, there had been more and more of them to mourn: the baby he had once been, the stumbling little figure of the one-year-old, the wild, dazzling brightness of the four-year-old, the five-year-old who had run towards her with arms outstretched. The black despair of the young adult, the twenty-year-old's brown jackets and cigarillos and hurrying steps away from her. All these shadows that she had been obliged to bury with him instead.

Next to the Gertrude Stein look-alike hung an ageing schoolboy who had proved to be surprisingly shy. When she addressed him he cast his eyes down to the stone floor and shuffled his shoe back and forth on the ingrained fossils. He wept with emotion when he spoke in the Society – he was heavy of heart like an old soldier – but he was also a convivial old soak who was crazy about dancing. On one occasion he had invited her for a boat ride and slowly they chugged along in the black water between the archipelago islands without either of them finding anything to say. Two custard slices and an increasingly tepid pot of coffee stood untouched at the stern waiting for them. Enthroned next to this gentleman – in a pale angel portrait – was the one who took his seven jealous siblings to all the functions. His siblings always sat in the front row, smouldering with love and envy. When he was worried, the flock trembled with him and collapsed as one man into his old neuroses. Meanwhile he was very fond of the portrait painter, his gaze was tender and vaguely erotic, and he was happy sitting for his portrait from dawn until dusk. During the breaks they romped around on the Thousand-and-One-Nights carpet like two jolly baby boys.

One of the ladies had her portrait painted with the Venus effect. At first you thought she was looking at herself in the mirror in boundless vanity, but then, like a bolt to the chest, came the discovery that it was *oneself* she was looking at, from the dizzying perspective of eternity. She was a lady who appeared to be very special, as ladies often do when they are in short supply in a gaggle of gentlemen. From time to time this lady dressed up and turned into a swan, swishing around in the world outside for a while, before returning to herself. Occasionally she would feel the iron grab of the lady's hand searching for hers under the table.

Next to the Venus lady hung another lady, the one who looked as though she wanted to retreat from every situation she found herself in. Like a worm she would creep away from the person she was talking to, as if she was guilty of something unforgivable that was about to impact on the world. She herself often wondered what fascinating white-collar crime might be involved. Hanging slightly apart were the portraits of the more anonymous gentlemen, the ones who were like the parrots travelling by car in Hitchcock's *The Birds*, leaning first this way and then that, depending on which way the car swerved, in this case according to the light current of air caused by the strong feelings blowing through the hall. Small compact bird bodies with a permanent slight lean, they could have had a group portrait, but they wanted their own.

On one occasion when they were sitting waiting for their new medals, the lady who sometimes turned into a swan squeezed her sweet-shaped handbag and asked if she might look inside.

"A sweet indeed . . ."

She realised it was somewhat inappropriate to be the owner of this worn-out sweet-shaped handbag, because she had learned that a woman's handbag was a direct reflection of her sexuality, but the lady chuckled fondly when she surveyed the paltry contents: a half-eaten crab, a shocking pink lipstick, a dead cat and an unknown volume by Thomas Mann.

"Surely you understand the inside of a lady's handbag can't look as pitiful as this?"

She nodded, she did understand, and the lady rang for a hackney cab, ordering the driver to take them to the nearest department store. Then they walked around inside the glittering vessel of goods. The lady stormed ahead like a torpedo and made the sales staff fish out one exclusive object after another. She left wearing a little fur jacket and a new shoulder bag in a much more fashionable style, which looked mediocre but cost a fortune, and the bag was now bursting with things that suggested beauty and cool genius. The adventure led to them missing their medals, but what did that matter? They would soon receive new ones. On the way home the lady took her hand, kissed it, and turned her extraordinary water-clear eyes to her.

"I would like to express my admiration for you as a person. You're a wild one, aren't you? I am too, but I'm a stickler for traditions. If you came to my home, you would understand. We can go straight there if you like."

"Maybe one day . . . ," she said. She, who always kept herself to herself, she, who always was the first to run home from parties and miss the secret conversations after alcohol had unmasked people's souls. Home she rushed as though there was someone waiting for her.

She perused the portraits with the portrait painter at her shoulder like a shadow.

"When may I paint you?"

"Later."

"I can paint you while you're asleep."

"Never."

She could picture the scene: collected from the apartment at night, carried off while she slept and placed on the stool, sitting there with lolling head while he dispatched her to eternity. She already had a feeling that she was in a dream. Details recurred in an odd and alarming way: she thought of someone she knew and the person would immediately appear, she made a note of something and then it flitted past as an item of news on the radio. Things were reiterated, duplicated and seemed all too easily connected.

"I can paint you whenever you like. I can paint you upside down or from the back or as God intended you. I can paint you with a crow. You're going to be very attached to your portrait, believe me. And I can see your soul fluttering in there. I would really like to have a go at capturing it."

She found it difficult to remember the gentlemen and the few ladies when she was sitting alone in her apartment during the week looking out over the awful ash tree. She counted them on her fingers, a bit like Snow White and the nameless dwarves, and when they saw one another again they were affectionate and obliging, lined up in their evening wear, clinking drinks, beaming at her, making another toast to her future. There were endless calls for a toast. They raised their antique glasses to one thing after another, and so they were an ebullient bunch. One moment they were raising a glass to her youth, the next to her achievements, and yet another to the aura of her womanhood, untainted by childbirth as it was. Generally speaking, copious amounts were drunk. It made her feel both at home and unhappy, as it had done in her old family, where they all got sloshed whenever they could. She missed the girls from the underworld who had formed her adolescence, some of whom were dead now, some living a life remote from her own. Her brother was with her wherever she went, despite grave, headstone, time, wind, eternity and the rest.

Every time she stepped through the portal in the years that followed, she thought about the gentlemen and the few ladies and the matter of their impending deaths. The agreement was that you only left the flock as a corpse, the idea being that you would be taken straight from a meeting to the morgue. She could constantly see before her the stretchers that would soon leave the palace bearing someone from among them. The day a member died, that person's portrait would be carried down to the large archives lying beneath them like a sepulchre and be laid on the hill of time. As for her, she sometimes longed for that day. Some of the chairs were already empty; they were the ones who had left the Society prematurely, run away, never to be heard of again. No-one knew where they were now, no-one spoke of those who were no longer there. Perhaps they had simply not wanted to be carried out of the fold headfirst. She was born several generations after them and that made her feel a special affection for them, they could have been her parents, or even her grandparents. She was both young enough and old enough for people to start informing her that there was still time for her to produce offspring. She had never wanted any and, being the last in a long line of lunatics and drunks, she regarded her tiny existence as a last barrier against an immense wave of darkness. She wanted her family's chaotic flame to die out with her, and it seemed to be in her nature to always up sticks, to leave everything behind her as though she were running away from a mighty forest fire. She had a single mission and she was loyal to that alone.

There were dark halls and weary muses, there were palace dinners, secrecies, autocracies, blood soup, dove soup. There were frenziedly twinkling chandeliers, there were grumbles and growls inside the paintings, there were doubles moving slowly through the halls, shy as bats in daylight. The perfumes in which they showered the Society before the functions were difficult to endure; the stench could last for weeks and when it had finally faded away it was time for them to be paraded again on the ever-revolving stage. The audience for the antics was half asleep and the Society's members fell into a deep slumber, reeling away in their dreams, dreams of times that no longer existed, of a fame that none of them really knew if they deserved. The emperor was the only one awake, blinking in the ceremonial light. But not everyone admired the Society; the kingdom was overflowing with dégagé technologists who raged the instant anyone used a word of more than two syllables. Books, paintings, pianos, oriental rugs had also had to emigrate from homes to out-of-town rubbish tips in favour of gadgets of various kinds. The aesthetic of the age and the home was that of the mortuary and the autopsy room. In this new age the Society looked slightly exotic and outmoded and there were far-reaching plans to move it all to the City Museum. But their work progressed: the gentlemen and the few ladies spent millions on the acquisition of a book from the Middle Ages, they purged the catalogues that were overrun with pests, they conserved the ancient objects, they had meetings with the emperor and the presiding officer and the Supreme Court. The emperor came sweeping in now and then with his sceptre, swinging it rather aimlessly in front of him, and then swept home again. As for her, she appreciated the slowness and inertia of the Society, resistant to the hungry tooth of time out there. She imagined that people with a book in their hand would soon exist only in moth-eaten old texts, and then the butterflies and birds would suffer the same fate, the beat of their wings existing only between the covers of a scholarly tome, and finally the extinct signs of man would only be found there too. She threw herself into her tasks, she wrote and tidied and arranged. She always ran all the way to the palace from the bleak apartment, often in circles she didn't understand herself, and even after many different seasons in the Society she occasionally managed to get lost in the boulevards and be late for a function, as if the street maps weren't quite right in this part of the city. And one winter afternoon, when the light was particularly soft, she finally sat down on the stool that actually belonged to the muses, and allowed herself to be immortalised in black oil. She sat still as a fly in front of the portrait painter while he painted, and inside her she felt vanity stir like a living being.

The portrait took its time. She placed herself at the portrait painter's disposal whenever he wished. She was used to handling both rogues and gods, especially when they happened to arrive in the same person. The painter's compliments during the sitting were both impertinent and fawning, weaselling their way under her clothes, but inside she had a place no-one could reach. For this reason her portrait wasn't going to be the greatest either: it was vacant and quite blurred, making her look as though she was at one with the night behind her, and she deserted her stool as often as she could. He adjusted her clothes while she sat, she hardly noticed, and on several occasions she had to rush out and buy a new accessory. A ruff, a feather, a pair of large earrings, a suitcase, a stuffed jackdaw, a rapier that had belonged to Richard III's valet.

"You are lovelier than the loveliest loveliness."

"Hesperian," Big Brother to the seven siblings corrected his portraitist and his mirror while he strutted around between the portraits.

"And tremendously intelligent."

She hated the word intelligent, it made her feel like a piece of livestock, and the portraitist could sniff out people's aversions.

"You brought a breath of dusky spring," he carried on, "and we like to linger in it."

Perhaps it was the little cat in her handbag that stank, or else it was her sex. A girl's sex was rotting from the start, smelling, glistening like a mussel even when she was young, and nothing in a woman aged with dignity.

She noticed that people gave a little bow in her presence now and, like the rest of the Society, she seemed to hover slightly above life, in a rather majestic way, somewhere in the realm between humans and gods. Her father rang and wrote to her from time to time, but she kept her silence next to the ash tree; she had nothing to say and it turned out he didn't either on the few occasions she answered. He was drunk and confused and made himself all the more impossible whenever he sought to make amends. He simply seemed guiltier every time he protested his innocence. She had always known he was a rogue, but now he had emerged as a fraudster with a criminal record too. She had thought he was entirely open with who he was – bombastic, unreliable, loveless – that there couldn't be anything else lurking underneath that was worse. Every time he rang her he chewed off a bit more of her soul. One evening she thought she could glimpse the guy with whom she had found the kitten, sitting right at the back in the audience during a function. Then he was standing under a streetlamp in the small square with the chestnut trees, but when she called from her window he hurried away. Some mornings a faint scent of the Atlantic lingered in the doorway.

It was still winter, all the trees were bare, and Bartók's night music was blaring through the halls. She stood in the ladies' room and examined her face after an evening devoted to Lethe and her tribulations in the world of the gods. A battle had long been waging in the Society about whether Lethe should be restored to the country's name day calendar. To be specifically associated with oblivion and lost items was not a worthy activity for a goddess of her calibre. Others thought they needed to give it some time, and a third view was that there was a certain kind of mythology beyond redemption. She felt the kitten in her handbag, just a thin skeleton now, a little outline of a kitten, but she liked it all the same. She had changed her dress eight times and she had been notified about which gentlemen she had been assigned for the evening. Since the gentlemen were many, the few ladies would circulate among them during the proceedings, and the ladies were duly requested to keep track of the little time card on which the evening's gentlemen were listed. First out this evening was a meek gentleman with whom she would be able to converse while thinking about something else, but after that it would get more difficult. The sullen ones were easiest; they sat staring at their own glum horizon. She could handle the conceited and the embittered as well. The hardest were the timid ones, those who really wanted to sit with other gentlemen. With them she had to make an effort to concoct conversational gambits and be charming. After dinner had been served, the gentlemen would scamper up to the Hall of Beauty, while she and the few ladies would sit half asleep for a while, clutching a draught of cognac, before they were collected by their separate hackney cabs. But now she was still waiting to sit down next to her meek table companion. The muses were there adjusting his ruff, which always seemed to end up askew and expose his chest through a gap. His formal attire was literally giving him the slip. A noisy minstrel screeched into her other ear.

"You are as fair as a floozy," bawled the portrait painter from the other side of the table, where he was bickering with the friend who would always be number one in the great band of siblings. On some evenings those two were allowed to sit together, gentleman and gentleman, to forestall any bleating and whining and long faces. Her table companion was now standing to attention beside her. She looked at the sparkling prisms of the chandelier as they waited for the fanfare to sound, watched the polished glass shoot little beams of light around it. And in a universe of contradictory laws of gravity that man was there to defy, where the gabardine was heavy and limp and slippery and the gentleman next to her was small and scrawny under his strained belly, suddenly, as luck would have it, he was standing next to her in his underpants. She averted her eyes, pretended to cough into the linen napkin and bent down to tighten the buckles on her high-heeled shoes. When, after a brief eternity, she dared to glance back, he was fully clothed again. The portrait painter leaned across the table, invigorated by the incident that afterwards seemed like a hallucination.

"You choose too often to be true to yourself."

"Are you sure?"

"Yes."

"Not I."

"You'll see."

As they waited for her reply the two gentlemen raised their glasses in a unison toast in her honour, while her table companion sat next to her with his trousers on, his cheeks flushed and an innocent smile on his lips.

She was perched on her stool with a trembling peacock feather in her hand. The portrait painter had requested a night-time session. Around them there was silence, just a faint breeze moving through the halls, and his armour-bearer and brother lay sleeping in a corner with a golden mantle over him. The mood was dark and still, the artist poked at his paints and she stretched to stay awake. The first few times she had sat here she had been afraid that something would be stolen from her, but she was no longer afraid, for she didn't want to keep any of what she was. She picked up the little cat skeleton and held it carefully in her hand. The painter raised an eyebrow and started splattering the paint faster; perhaps it was a little corpse the portrait had been missing. A bevy of rowdy ghosts drifted past in the next hall, deceased members of the Society who couldn't stay away. She waved at them as they drank and recited and waved back, crestfallen, scrupulous as they were over etiquette and precedence.

"Are you a happy person?" asked the painter, sucking on the end of the paintbrush.

"I don't think so."

He smiled and his face split in two, one half mournful and the other full of joy.

"No. Who has time to be happy? I'm sure I've never come across a happy person. I meant more whether you enjoy being here."

"Enjoyment is for softies."

They fell silent for a while as the paintbrush scratched and scraped in his hand.

"Are you sorry you came here?" he said in the end.

"No."

She stretched out her arm, which was cold from sitting still for so long.

"And you?"

"You have no notion of where I was before."

She looked down at her legs sticking out under the dress, the stumpy ankle disappearing into the short boot. How many times had she changed her footwear this evening? How many dresses had she slipped on and off since she came here? When she was young she had loved studying her body, its precision, its perfection. It was not that she was more precise and perfect than anyone else, nor that she could take advantage of this supposed beauty, since she was shy and timid, but everything was still intact and unspoilt, it was soft and firm at the same time, like a godly formula in her hands. When her stepmother had stood in the bathtub washing her colossal purple-brown loins, where the pubic hair hung in strands like on a cow, she had watched in fascination, looked at all the lathering and splashing around the wretched thing between her legs and wondered if she would have one of those herself one day. The painter lowered his brush. It was starting to grow light outside and she thought she might have fallen asleep for a while without noticing.

"I think I can continue painting without your presence now."

She – the main person in this little story, you can imagine many others – continued to do her job, carried on documenting and cataloguing the precious objects of which she was custodian. In the spring, when there was a particularly large amount to do in the Society – polishing the sculptures, overhauling the drawbridge – she testified to the police against her father, making her statement discreetly over the telephone from the palace. She was told she didn't need to testify: that was what the law said in regard to daughters and fathers. She replied that she no longer had a father, that she was tired of charlatans and charmers, delinquents and drinkers, that she had spent a lifetime with them and always defended them, but this time he would have to manage as best he could in the legal system. And then she made her statement, slightly distracted by the shadowboxing of the two gentlemen next to her, but it was a distraction she thanked the gods for. Her father was taken in for questioning and thrown into the Remand Centre, since they suspected he would try to flee to one of his lovers abroad. The old gods were falling, such was the time, but they would bounce back – they always did. She had worried about her father her whole life, invented an imaginary father in his stead, treasured pretty sparks from his many fires.

All tragedies end in death, it is said, and all comedies end in marriage, but this is a story without a natural ending. Death wouldn't take her for some time, so it seemed, and marriage sounded more arduous than going to war. The portrait was finished. After experimenting with several props and costumes, the painter had depicted her with a toy sword and a man's hat in pink, and the little cat manifested itself as a brooch on her cape. In the background he had outlined a vast troll forest and beyond a few pine trees standing alone was a glimpse of the sea in the distance. The portrait was hung beside the others. The portrait painter said he would kill himself if she didn't adore it. She said she adored it. A comet flew past their exhausted planet, brushing against it with its glowing tail. Her old and new families lived within her like a band of robbers.

A few more members of the Society had gone into exile and settled among the eternal youths in Rotterdam. Others had literally gone underground and now belonged to the free circle of the dead. The meek one, whose formal attire had escaped him, went down for embezzlement, but since evil is more seductive and distinctive and persuasive than goodness, this transgression added more glory to the strange association. Her father had succeeded in charming the magistrate just as he had charmed people his entire life, and he was back in front of the television, an ever shifty shadow in her life. She discovered that old explanations had merely created new mysteries. How long did something last, for example, that was called forever? What was an empire actually? She observed that she had started to communicate with the world around her only in hour-long speeches written down in advance. She noticed that she had lost all her friends and that she didn't miss any of them. She noted yet again that she missed the one who was cut out for life, the one with whom she had gone to Agadir. She always would, but she knew that she would leave him again and again if he came back; it was an impulse inside her she couldn't help. Now he was one of the anonymous faces in the city that had nothing to do with her. One evening when she walked up to her front door, someone had written BREAK WITH YOUR FATHERS in paint on the front of the building. She didn't know who had left the message, but she knew it was directed at her, and she broke with her father.

She stood in the hall with the paintings, where some of the sculptures had toppled over and lay in pieces on the floor. Dust and ashes swirled around in the air. The window where the little bronze head had its place was open to the street; a tune could be heard outside and the head that had looked at her mistrustfully so many times seemed to be smiling faintly against the light. Summer had arrived out there and the air streaming in through the window was smooth as silk. She removed the wig and placed it on the little bronze head. She wrote down a short but very polite farewell letter and walked up to the painting that portrayed herself. She had often felt alone in this room, she had felt very much loved, and she had learned things about people and about herself that she wouldn't have wanted to be without. She had liked the many afternoons in the motionless light where scratching pens and little sighs were all that could be heard. She had sometimes felt she had to protect the flock from themselves, for most of them were only vaguely conscious of time rushing past outside. In here a different measure of time prevailed, and different laws: the laws of beauty and poetry and ancient chivalry. She stood for a moment looking at her own slightly ghostlike figure in the painting, the dark bob, the sword in her hand, and she longed for the ocean glinting in the distance beyond the trees. And with one step she disappeared inside the oily blackness.

MY PSYCHOANALYST

His voice always seemed to come from inside me when he was sitting in his armchair behind my head.

"But she's my child, after all," he said.

"Child?" I said. "She's an adult, your daughter. Thirty-two, as far as I'm aware."

"How do you know that?"

"The internet . . . Just say you like me more than her. Just say it, then we can move on."

Behind me he smiled, I could hear it. Sometimes I made him laugh out loud. That was the best part.

"It's impossible to compare the two of you. You know that."

"Because I'm out of her league?"

He smiled again. When someone sits behind your back you learn to hear the slightest movement and expression.

"You have children yourself."

"Don't drag them into this."

Birds were flying around outside, the view was dismal, industrial. With every change of venue, the place we met had become slightly simpler. First the grand apartment near Humlegården, then the large room on Olof Palmes gata, looking out onto Norra Bantorget, and lastly here, a little dump in Fruängen. It suited us both and it felt increasingly as though I was visiting him in a personal capacity. The couch was small, it was a divan like any other, and I felt like Goldilocks going to lie on a bed in a strange man's house three times a week. I often imagined he was sitting behind my head masturbating, which I suppose said more about me than him, unfortunately. It was a fear that I never really overcame, but we learned to live with it during the seven years I went to see him. He looked like a jaded Freud, with friendly pale-blue eyes and a faint air of tragedy about him. For me it was important that he shouldn't be unhappy, that he had his house in order, but a person without some level of disorder is not to be found in this world; you have to perfect the art of tolerating your own and other people's shortcomings. He gently rustled something behind me, the ever-present mint pastilles. I wanted him to sit perfectly still so that I didn't need to be afraid of him.

"Maybe we should talk about something else now. The time will soon be up."

I was silent a moment and then I said:

"She seems to be a really smug bitch, your daughter, anyway."

He laughed aloud.

"She definitely is. And I'm delighted about that."

I went to visit a friend in Vienna so I had a few days off. It was already summer in Vienna. We strolled around in the elegant city that was still resting on stolen Jewish treasures. We went to the Freud museum and I took a picture of Freud's hat and sent it to my psychoanalyst; anything else would have felt like misconduct on my part. He replied that Freud had a habit of throwing his hat over especially fine mushrooms when he was out picking champignons in the forests around Lake Lavarone. To tell the truth, my psychoanalyst was sick of Freud and psychoanalysis: he had moved on to Buddhism, and from there to Hinduism, and finally into a landscape even more mystical. Every time I was there, he tried to persuade me to take up contemplation and prayer. The last year I was going to him he had become interested in the afterlife and sometimes, when I was sad, he consoled me with eternity.

"But can't we concentrate on this life?" I said, having turned to psychoanalysis to untangle my own life on earth. I thought that *this life* was a reasonable limit on our activities.

He brooded for a moment over a classic question to counter mine, before I heard a quiet "OK" behind me.

My friend, who had been in Vienna for ten years, lived in a poky apartment in Leopoldstadt. We borrowed an old Volvo and drove along the Danube. The small villages beside the river appeared to be sleeping in the shadow of the huge mountains. For long stretches there was no-one to be seen, just the dark, wide river flowing along next to us and looking as though it was going to burst its banks in places. Every so often one of those big boats filled with European pensioners slid past. Standing on deck and waving blithely, they looked like people who had no idea what they were supposed to be doing with their lives. My friend didn't drive very well and it was a bit jerky going through the city, but now we were driving gently along the river. There was some kind of klezmer music playing on the radio when he turned it on. The villages we drove past were so quiet it was surreal. I started thinking that we and the Volvo had been transported back to a time before the war. There was something so enduring about those mountains, and that thought made the landscape look even more dreamlike and forlorn. We were hungry and restaurant signs had started to spring up, but neither of us wanted to stop and eat anything here. Both wars had started here long before they officially broke out, beginning in the nightmares that haunted people. They dreamed they were hiding in piles of bodies, dreams that later proved to be ominously prophetic, in the same sense that the Second World War was hardwired into the Treaty of Versailles. Freud had left Vienna in June 1938. The villages here looked like they did then: sleepy, quiet, and the people were the same.

When I was living in Alsace as a young student I sometimes cycled to the German border in Karlsruhe with my French friends. We would cross the bridge over the Rhine and we were suddenly in Germany. One night when I was slightly drunk and in a strange state – it was difficult to judge whether it was happiness or unhappiness – I cycled to the river on my own after a party. On the French side I walked down to the riverbank with the vague notion of swimming across to Germany. I was walking around, feeling quite exhilarated, when I saw an otter. It was sitting absolutely still on the silty, litter-strewn strip of mud. Our eyes met and locked. I sat down at the river's edge and we carried on looking at each other. I was surprised at the humanity in its gaze, the small consciousness inside the grey animal that was just like mine. We stayed there until it was light. I climbed back up to my bicycle and when I looked down from the bridge I saw the otter slip soundlessly into the water and drift out into the river. But now we were driving along a different river, the Danube. My friend was tired, feeling old, he said. I had never asked him how old he was, but his eyes were still young – they always would be.

"What do you want to do with the rest of your life?" I said.

"No idea," he said. "What about you?"

"Me neither."

We drove along the Danube and when we returned to Vienna everything around us was dark. This was the sort of thing I would tell my psychoanalyst when I next saw him, disconnected events and episodes without meaning. My friend in Vienna kept a candle burning all night while he slept under his crucifix. Both of us wondered whether we should use the opportunity to fall in love, but it was as if neither of us had the energy for it. We were both a bit too fed up with ourselves, but I was happy he was my friend. When the plane the next day made a sudden turn over the Danube and we were hanging at an angle in the sky, I wasn't afraid like I once would have been. I knew my friend was travelling along in the train below me, a single flash of silver across the landscape, back into the city and the small apartment. And more than a thousand kilometres further north my psychoanalyst was sitting in his armchair, waiting for me as though nothing else in the world existed for him.

*

The masturbation thing was a recurrent problem for us. At the slightest movement in his armchair behind me, I panicked, and that made him feel uncomfortable. Like all psychoanalysts, he hoped I would become infatuated with him. That I only associated him with the flashers and sex offenders of my childhood meant that his little halo had slipped. If he intended to stand up to open the window, he was always obliged to ask me if he could. Even so, I sometimes fell asleep while I was lying there, and he would let me sleep. Once when I awoke a cloud was about to float in through the window. I was going to mention it to him, and I raised my hand in the air to point, but then I fell asleep again and when I woke up it was gone. I was often angry with him and railed at him. Sometimes he was angry with me as well, but his patience was admirable. He had certainly been paid for putting up with me, but I am not sure I would have been prepared to be lambasted every week for a few tenners.

"Coming here will make you neither healthy nor free," he had often said back then, at the beginning, "and it won't make anything stop hurting."

I had no such expectations, but I kept going there, bowing to his theories and to him, an unfamiliar older man about whom I knew nothing. It was as if I was practising bowing to my fate, putting up with life always turning out the way it did.

The daughter was also a recurrent problem. Some things he did tell me about himself: that his own psychoanalyst had committed suicide, that he had lost his twin sister as a child, that his daughter kept a certain distance from him.

"You spend more time with me than with her. Have you thought about that?" I said.

I heard him reckoning up in his head.

"Yes."

"Do you wish I was your daughter instead?"

He was silent, fiddling with something.

"Well?" I said.

He cleared his throat.

"I have to answer no to that question."

"You don't have to do anything. It'll stay between us. And that bitch will never find out you think I'm more fun than her."

He laughed.

"Well, in that case."

I paused for a moment, listening for more.

"Was that a confession?"

"I don't think so. How would it be if you were my daughter?"

"I'd be as annoyed with you as I am now."

"And what else?"

I couldn't think of anything to say.

"Aren't you really a bit too old to be in need of a father? It's a long time since you needed one."

I considered it. Where would I even keep a father? Would I start visiting him and his wife in Sundbyberg?

"Yes, I suppose I am," I said. "She can have you."

"That's a blessing."

I thought of my own children, how they always stood out in a crowd of other children, their faces sharply chiselled in life's grey and meaningless milling around. I saw only them, their bright eyes and soft cheeks. Their small friends, who sauntered in and out of our house, appeared drab and hard to love. I used to think that I would always have missed my children if I had produced any others. If I hadn't had children with Jonas, I would always have known that my real children existed somewhere else, trapped in time. We were part of a baby group after our daughter was born and Jonas and I used to say to each other afterwards that the others in the group were always stealing a rueful glance at our child; they were obviously disappointed in their own babies.

"She's not as special as you think," I said to my psycho-analyst now.

"Maybe not," he said, "but she doesn't have to be special. It's enough that she exists."

The psychoanalyst's daughter turned out to be loosely connected with my line of work, making a slow but irritating little career on the periphery of my life. Basically I wanted to outlaw her from our field and ensure she was barred. For a period – it was when I was frequently living in hotels for my work – we would occasionally end up at the same event in Copenhagen. I was scared of sleeping alone, so travelling was difficult for me. The fear always came at night: I was clinging on to the back of the world like a starving animal and was never coming back. I had to push the furniture in front of the window to stop myself from jumping. When day finally rescued me, I was like an old ghost and it sometimes felt as though those nights lasted a thousand years. It was when I went down for breakfast on one of those mornings that I saw her at a table a short distance away. She wasn't nearly as full of herself as I had imagined. She looked small behind her large breakfast. Later that day I was alone in the hotel lobby with a glass of wine when she came in through the glazed doors. She walked up to me, introduced herself and said she admired my work and then she told me a little about hers. "Self-righteous cunt," I thought to myself, and put on the beaming smile that usually gets me what I want. I didn't say anything to my psychoanalyst about us bumping into one another. I wanted something meatier if I was going to talk about it.

"Did you enjoy Copenhagen?" he asked when I was back.

"Not particularly. I don't like travelling. It's the same wherever you go. People. Buildings. Time. Money."

"But you're always travelling."

"Yes."

The next time we saw each other was exactly a year later when there was another convention in Copenhagen, with the same suspects who always showed up, like going to a class reunion. For once I went to one of the end-of-day parties. There she was again, her hair a fraction longer, her spectacles larger. Everyone's spectacles had got bigger that year, as if there had been a decree from above, and I felt the same burning hatred as I had the previous year. She was rather tipsy, dancing coquettishly on the spot, and after a while she approached me. She said again that she admired me and told me what had been happening to her since we last met. She was not the only one to gratuitously produce her mediocre CV the moment anyone asked for the time, but she and her persona were more infuriating than most.

"Cunt Vernacular," I said to myself.

I was given yet another résumé of the last year. I listened and I put on my beaming smile. Then I said I had to go and ring my children.

It was early summer and I was lying on the couch again. We were talking about the Nazi, as we often did. We had a minor cast of characters to which we returned, some of them predictable, others rather more surprising, peripheral figures who had skirted past my life and somehow stuck to me. The Nazi and I had attended the same secondary school. In my eyes he had been smart, scholarly and stunning, and I had felt like an idiot next to him. We had seen each other once or twice, at home on my mum's sofa drinking beer, visiting the Prins Eugen Museum. After school he had a meteoric rise as one of the intelligentsia, a career which a few years later had derailed into Nazism. From having been an intellectual star he was cast out to the margins. Now he went on marches with European Nazis and made underground radio broadcasts while he was drunk. Meanwhile I had gradually made a name for myself, also in intellectual circles, but I would forever have the feeling that I had stolen his place in the world, that he had ended up in the swamp in my stead. My psychoanalyst laughed.

"What are you laughing at?"

"I can see you marching along the streets with the Nazis."

"Me too. A little Nazi pin-up girl. But I don't know if I would have been there. It was more that I took his place in the world."

My psychoanalyst rose from the armchair and as usual I froze. He sat down again.

"I'm sorry. I was just going to switch on the fan."

I met his daughter one last time. Another year had passed and it was also the last time I went to Copenhagen. I was divorced by now and I missed my children more when I was away from home than when I was in my cold apartment waiting for them. I saw her from a distance in the crowd. I rang my friend in Vienna from the hotel and asked him what I should do. He sounded happy to hear my voice.

"Well, what would you like to do with her?"

"Get rid of her."

He laughed. I liked his laugh; it was always completely unguarded. He giggled like a kid.

"What are you doing?" I said.

"Driving. Along the Danube."

"On your own?"

"No."

"With a woman?"

"Mmm."

"Ah."

I could see him there in the Volvo with a shadow by his side, driving onwards in his awkward lurching fashion.

"We just stopped and ate sauerkraut and sausage. A wonderful little lunch place."

The presence of the woman beside him must have had an effect not just on him, but on the whole landscape. I heard the lightness in his voice, the gentle rush of air from an open window, her headscarf fluttering in the wind.

"So you want to get rid of her?" he said.

"Oh, it was nothing," I said and hung up.

The last time I was at my psychoanalyst's I sat opposite him on a chair like a normal adult. I had only done that a few times over the years, when we had fallen out and he had forced me to sit up and look him in the eye. When I had started going to him, I had collected some pictures of fathers which I took to show him. An odd bunch. Andy Warhol. Alfred Hitchcock. Vladimir Nabokov. Bas Jan Ader, who disappeared in the Atlantic in 1975 from his boat, the *Ocean Wave*. Efraim Longstocking, father of Pippi. And an unknown young man in a trench coat on a bicycle. Typical of me, to choose the impossible ones, the ones who had gone up in smoke or were slightly insane, like Nabokov, who only wanted to drive around the roads with the back seat full of the butterflies he had caught. The pictures now lay on the table between us. I picked them up one by one and looked at them. Bas Jan Ader had been caught by the camera at the precise second he let go of a tree branch and fell into a canal in Amsterdam. Hitchcock had an enormous cigar in his mouth and on this mighty cigar sat a small black bird that was about to fly off.

"I like this one," he said and pointed to Hitchcock.

"I do too," I said. "Do you remember when we smoked cigars?"

"I'll never forget."

"Was that actually allowed?"

He thought for a moment.

"Yes, it was."

"Do you remember what we were celebrating?"

"Not really."

"I remember. I was in love. But then I got over it. He was married, so it didn't work out well."

"And you were also married, if I remember correctly."

"Yeah."

The day I had smoked my cigar on the couch and he his in the armchair, the window had been open to the summer and the sound of whistling steamboats in the distance. The smoke had slowly risen and formed a false ceiling of silky grey above us.

"I was a bit jealous of you then," he said now.

His eyes were soft.

"Were you?"

"Yes. You were so full of life. I wanted to be young again when I saw you."

I had been young when I had come to see him the first time, and now I was no longer young. It was wonderful. It was our seventh summer and the window was open to the sky.

"Was I OK as a patient?" I asked.

"You were more than that."

"Even though I almost never wept and just argued with you and thought you were sitting there wanking the whole time?"

"Exactly."

His eyes were like rainfall, both happy and sad at the same time. When I looked at him then, I didn't know I would come across his obituary in the newspaper a few months later. The little alarm clock on the table confirmed it was time to go.

"And you do know all psychoanalysts are failed maniacs and psychopaths?"

He smiled.

"Definitely. You've told me."

"How's your daughter, by the way?"

"She's fine. She's just had a baby."

"And you're a grandfather?"

"Yes."

"Hmm. You still like her a bit more than me, don't you?"

He was silent. Silences were his speciality. They could last for a small eternity, and sometimes it drove me mad, but not now. I stood up and put on my thin jacket.

"Anyway, I have a farewell present for you."

He also rose from his chair, somewhat more stiffly than he had seven years previously, and I stood before him one last time.

"Don't you want to know what it is?"

"Of course I do."

He leaned forward and looked behind me as if a gigantic package with shiny paper and a red bow should suddenly appear next to my chair.

"My present to you is that I shall try to stay in the light from now on."

WE WERE BEASTS OF PREY

One day she was just sitting there on the back seat when I woke up from my doze. Her short legs were sticking straight out, she was wearing an old-fashioned cloak and she had a locket that was hanging down to her tummy.

"Hello," I said.

She didn't answer, merely stared ahead at her shoes, which were incredibly small and pink, tied like ballet slippers, with the appearance of moccasins. I glanced at my father in the rearview mirror, but he had his eyes on the road as if he were alone in the car.

There was a suitcase between us on the seat, garishly red and shiny. When she noticed I was gazing at it, she laid a hand on the smooth leather as if to stop me prying into her world, then she glowered out of the streaked window again, though there was nothing to see out there. Rain-laden trees, endless greenery that changed all the time, dense as rainforest in places, a greenness assuming the form of fir trees here, of spindly teenage birches over there. The little being had freckles and her hair hung down her back. It was black and glossy as silk. It looked as though someone had brushed it recently and tied back the strands around her face into a little topknot on the back of her head. Someone who wanted her to look nice, someone who cared. I remembered the sensation of my mother's hands in my hair, of their slow movements as she loosened the twists and tangles. The little girl smelled unfamiliar, and as she sat there, tiny and stoic and proud, she felt as alien as the creatures and half-humans of the forest. I wasn't sure whether she was a miniature person or a very small child. The clothes were not the kind children wore, at least not children from my century. Formal and stiff.

It was drizzling outside, a gentle, innocent summer rain, and the unknown girl's cape was wet. It had rained for days and the water formed a wall between us and the landscape. We sat in silence, listening to the sound of raindrops falling on sheet metal, at least I was, and I noticed that she didn't like me watching her and she behaved as if the car was hers, as if she had always been sitting there looking pompous. I continued to stare into the rearview mirror in search of answers, but my father was following the road with his eyes half-closed; the purr of the engine usually made him drowsy. Once in a while I would drive for a stretch and let him sleep. Our car was easy to handle, gliding through the landscape like vapour.

"Who are you?" I asked, a little louder, to command some respect.

"I don't know," she said, sticking her little nose up in the air.

"But maybe you have a name and come from somewhere?"

"It would be a matter of my own concern if I did."

She was too young for phrases like *a matter of my own concern*, but she didn't realise. A person's name couldn't be secret, after all. She could be a Dora or an Olivia or a Florence, but that wouldn't tell me why she was sitting here on the seat next to me. She raised her thin, translucent hand and drew a figure in the condensation on the car window.

"What's that?"

"A monkey."

"Oh."

"You can see that, can't you? It's a chimpinzee."

I didn't correct her pronunciation, because I didn't want to get involved in an argument with a stranger, I just wanted her to disappear. We gazed out of our respective windows at the rain still making everything grey and blurred, and when the car came to a stop on the verge, my father turned and looked at us, smiling.

"May I introduce . . . your sister."

"I don't have a sister," I said.

"You do now. Isn't she cute?" my father said, and we contemplated her as with a single eye. She blushed, slowly, and, to tell the truth, I had never seen anything cuter, but I didn't say so. She looked like a doll, or a flower.

"Does she have a name?"

"I'm called Johnny, if you must know."

"What sort of name is Johnny for a girl?"

"That's the thing about you two," my father said, "one's cuter than the other."

The rain was falling harder out there, as if the whole world were dissolving. The downpour was making the car clean and when it stopped a new landscape would be revealed, wide, cleansed, green, newborn. Johnny's cloak and hair were wet and it looked as though she had come close to drowning out there. We had a battery-driven fan for the summer, which was usually in the back with me when the heat arrived. Some days the car was unbearable without it.

"I can help you dry your clothes, if you like," I said, and dug it out from under all the things on the floor – clothes and objects we had bought with the intention of possibly selling later, a globe, a stethoscope, a mannequin, crockery, stuffed animals – but her little hand clutched the neck of her cape and she shook her head vigorously. She wanted to carry on being wet and strange. My father started the car without saying anything more and we continued through the rain. The same old music came pouring out of the radio, a Magic Tree air freshener swung in time to the melody.

We had stopped along a road that wound its way through a birch forest, where everything was clear and glistening after the rain. The little interloper trod cautiously through the grass in her tiny shoes. She was very pale and still didn't want to talk to me. She spoke to my father as if they knew one another, which they must have done, somehow, if she was my sister. Between the trees there was a glimpse of a lake.

"My girls," my father said, flinging out his arms, "say that you've missed one another."

He laid out two towels and a bar of soap at the point where the trees met the lake and told us to wash. Then he disappeared into the forest. The lake was filled to the brim after the rain, and was overflowing between the birches here and there. Behind the cloud striations a pale sun winked like a drunken eye. No shore, just forest that eventually merged into water, and you could sit at the edge on a little grassy spur and dip your feet in. The water gleamed, a mirror to the unknown, fir trees that looked as though they were descending towards the lake and the quivering shape of my face, all distorted by the faint motion and, in reality, as alien to me as Johnny and the fuzzy blurs of faces flashing past in oncoming cars.

Every time I swam out in a lake I thought it was for the last time, but then I always swam back. In every sea and lake there is a draw you have to fight against; you have to kick your way back to land. My father used to stand on the shore, waiting, and I suppose I didn't want to disappoint him. Now I had this strange, silent girl with me. She quickly took off her cloak and dress, but she kept on her underclothes, and so I did too. And then we slipped down into the water; I went first and she followed. The water was cold and soft against the skin. I had forgotten to ask if she could swim, and apparently she couldn't, because when I turned, she had vanished. In a brief second the shiny surface had closed around its prey. I dived down after her, and in the quivering glint of the shifting world down there I saw her sinking, an expression of astonishment on her face and her hair floating upwards over her head, a falling anemone in the yellow water, and I thought I should let her go to the bottom and then I would have the back seat to myself. We observed each other in this silent world where no time existed, just this extended *nothingness*. It felt as though she could already read my thoughts, and in those thoughts she sank to the slimy bottom and banged into it and settled there like a doll in a natural grave. The astonished expression had gone and her face was blank now, neutral and still, as if she really didn't care whether I pulled her up or let her disappear into the sludge. Wide-open eyes, filled with water, no will, no wish. If she had demanded my help, it would have been easier to let her sink, it wouldn't have been my fault that she couldn't swim and became one with the mud, and nobody would miss such a strange little person as this, but I couldn't endure the blankness and indifference. I swam a few strokes and as I grabbed hold of her, time started moving again, surging forward as it did sometimes, and I swam towards the light and managed to get her up above the surface and pull her onto land. She vomited silt and lake water and old food, and when I saw her retch and cough I had a sudden feeling of tenderness and grudging admiration. Admiration for the way she refused to ask for help when she really needed it, tenderness for the heaving little back, the shoulder blades protruding like wings. Her feet were minute, like everything else about her, and she had a birthmark on her thigh. I also had a birthmark.

"Again," she said, and wiped her mouth with the discarded dress lying on the grass like a pink blossom.

"What do you mean, again?"

"I want to swim again."

Swim was what she had *not* done, but she was obviously tougher than I had thought.

"It didn't go very well last time. Have you forgotten already?"

She rose to her feet and stood in front of me, her white vest and knickers streaked with mud and some chicken spew still on her chin. Her green eyes gazed at me, water in them still, viridescent with a hint of yellow, shades of the mud, of the dark, amber light down there.

"Come on then."

Some of the trees had toppled over headfirst into the lake, felled by weight or thirst. And so I stood on one of those underwater trees, holding her under the arms, while her arms and legs lashed out in rapid succession in an approximation of swimming. When I let go, her body sped away as if someone had fixed a propellor under her stomach. It was a kind of doggy paddle with her arms beating up and down in front of her, but she didn't sink.

"You *can* swim! Could you do it all along?"

She looked at me with water in her eyes and smiled, for the first time since I'd met her. She became someone else when she smiled, a befreckled creature of light in the black water. It was addictive and later I would do anything to recapture that smile. Now it was clear that she was a child: a row of milk teeth, tiny as pearls, in a pink gum, the roseate sheen of childhood about her. She dipped down like a duckling and when she came back up she was still smiling.

We bathed for a long time and when we came out, my father was sitting there, waiting. We wrung out our hair and walked back to the road. She dozed off as soon as she had fastened her seatbelt, and she looked dead when she was sleeping, inanimate. Her head had slipped to one side, her mouth was slightly open. My father sought my eye in the rearview mirror.

"She's like you."

She wasn't, but I didn't say anything.

"I'm her dad."

"Yes, you said."

"I've been thinking for a long time that you need a sister. You should've had one ages ago. You're far too lonely here with me."

I wasn't. I didn't need a sister, but I didn't say so. I had never uttered a thousandth of what I had inside me. All the same, in the dazed state in which we drove around I was always half-comatose and her arrival had woken something inside me. We had never had any relatives, or at least none that we had met. They were all dead or had emigrated. Most of them had followed the crowds and left, sailing away over the ocean aboard luxury liners that no-one used anymore. Some were in South America and the occasional letter would arrive from there. It had been years since any letters had arrived from my mother, but each time we came to a new town, I hoped. But how could she know where we were? We never stopped anywhere for long. In the past I had left messages for her along our path. A Pink Panther top she had given me, a small Bible, a pair of my favourite tights. Now I didn't have anything left from her time. I had grown out of everything and was becoming a different person, hiding it all under men's clothes that were a bit too large. I was thinking of handing down my outgrown dresses to Johnny, the ones that weren't strewn like ulcers on the landscape we had travelled across several years before. A new era had begun when my mother disappeared and in this new era there was no time, no order, no rules. It was blank, gliding, non-temporal. In the beginning I had counted the days, but then I stopped. The lines on the wall in our old apartment were still there. Time started moving again with Johnny's arrival and suddenly it lurched forward in staccato bursts, uncertain and unchecked.

She looked tired when she woke, small creases and bags under her eyes. Children shouldn't look tired; they should be either lively as mice or asleep. Her little mouth opened and closed until she said,

"Where are we actually going?"

"Nowhere," I said. "You need to see this though."

I showed her the jar in which I had trapped a dragonfly. The thin, rainbow-coloured wings made it vibrate and a faint whirring noise could be heard through the glass. Her eyes widened.

"May I hold it?"

"If I get to look inside your locket."

"No-one can."

"No-go then."

I grew accustomed to the little character sitting next to me, looking out of the window. Summer arrived with its heat, sweeping everything away. Thoughts became more sluggish, days more torrid, nights more fleeting, and after a while it was as though she had always been sitting there. Soon it was difficult to recall a time before her, when my father and I had been alone in the car. I showed her my entire collection in the car boot of glass jars containing dead animals. I lent her my net and when she managed to catch a butterfly and, later, a bird in flight, she laughed.

"Shall we let the bird eat the butterfly now?" she asked. We watched the bird kill the butterfly in the glass jar and then we watched the bird die.

*

Sometimes, when she turned her face and looked at me from an infinite distance, I imagined she was several hundred years old and had always existed. But often when she was sitting there, short and glum and limp as a doll, slumped in the seat, you could see she was a little kid. I didn't like children. I usually gave them a wide berth, and their questions and their inquisitiveness when they flocked around the car every time we reached a new town. I didn't want anything to do with them, perhaps because they reminded me of myself, but our midnight-blue jalopy drew them to us, wherever we might have casually parked, be it by a church or a railway station. They pressed their faces to the windows like fish against the glass in an aquarium, but I didn't look up from my book. My father would open both front doors and let them prod their stubby fingers at the dashboard.

"Where do you come from?"

This was in the time when everyone came from somewhere; it wasn't like nowadays, when no-one can keep track of everyone's origin and history.

"We come from all over," my father said, and I wanted to ask where all over was.

We travelled on through the summer. This was the summer of 1982 and I would soon be fourteen. My father seemed tired behind the wheel and I would often talk to him to prevent him falling asleep. I lit a cigarette and held it out to him. The little person who was now a part of our life was sleeping beside me, stretched out on the seat on her stomach with her hands under her head.

"Is she really my sister?" I asked.

"Do you remember Blanche and the others?"

Blanche and her friends had whirled into the car and made it very crowded, but wonderful, and the smell of perfume wrapped us in something soft and full of promise. They drank from their small pocket flasks, but it didn't make them drunk, or else they were drunk already, quick, affectionate and quite scatterbrained and smiling.

"What are you reading?" Blanche would ask, running her finger along the top line in my book. I told her what I was reading and she listened intently as I explained the plot. Now when I think about myself, I seem hopelessly verbose and precocious, but Blanche looked at me with her curious eyes, eyes that never judged or rejected, and said I was a bookworm and a sweetheart. It may have been that I leaned against her on one such evening and nodded off for a while. Her breathing was fast and she always held a cigarette in her hand from which a thin, blue, minty smoke rose to the roof. It was as if she had shot an arrow that had travelled through time until now, when Johnny came to us.

It was a greeting from Blanche, which made me happy. I had been sad when she disappeared.

Our father's name was John, but no-one ever called him Johnny. He was John, and nothing else. John, like the John Silver cigarettes I had started smoking with him. John, like Follow John, the Follow My Leader game we used to play when Mother was still around and the three of us went collecting shells on the beach. John, like John Blund the sandman who took me with him to the land of sleep each night and then brought me back. John, like the anonymous figure who picked up girls such as Blanche at night, as if they were toys. Blanche must have called the girl Johnny so that she would never forget her father, and then she had dumped her here. Now John was all she had. I realised she looked like Blanche; she had the same high forehead and the same dead-straight hair, as if someone had ironed it. Shining hair that slipped and slid through your fingers. Mine was matted and unkempt and bleached after many days spent hanging out of the car windows. Sometimes, when I pretended to be asleep, I heard them talking, and it didn't sound the same as when I was awake. There was an intimacy between them I had never shared with my father, an invisible bond. I was my mother's child and I had never established a true attachment to him, even though I lived in his car. John had a sugary, syrupy voice when he spoke with her. And I was overwhelmed with blind jealousy. I had never bothered about him and yet he was mine, and he and his car were all I had in the world. When I saw the two of them sitting and chatting in the misty blue afternoon light, I thought that she had taken my place now, and soon I would be standing on the verge with my glass jars, hoping that someone would take pity on me.

Johnny had crept forward onto the seat next to him and she was laughing as he spoke. I had never laughed like that, I had always been the serious one, the one who could crush any festive mood with a mere narrowing of her eyes. Blanche had said it too. "Why so serious, little fly?" John was a master of creating that hypnotic party spirit on the margins of reality. It was his way of refusing to accept what kind of life he led. For everyone around him it was like being caught in a crazy, extended hallucination. Sometimes I thought I had simply dreamed that Johnny was sitting in the front with him, having a conversation, because I fell asleep every time and when I roused, she was back beside me.

I woke up because the car was standing still and they had gone. The engine was on and the windscreen wipers were still going, as if an alien force had whisked them both away while I slept. I was frightened, thinking they had left me for good, but when I shouted I saw them emerge at the edge of the forest, my father carrying her as she slept in his arms. He made a face at me to keep quiet. He laid her on the back seat and she continued to sleep, her breathing light as a feather and steady, and we drove on through a world that seemed without limit, the roads never ending and the landscape immutable. No matter how far we journeyed, it all remained the same – you carry within you a world that lies on top of the new world like a thin sheet.

A new age began. They were often gone when I woke and every time my father came back with her asleep, as if on each occasion in the forest he collected a new Johnny, a chrysalis that opened on the back seat as a replacement for the old one. He carried her the same way as the first time I saw them, hanging in his arms like an overgrown baby whom he placed on the back seat without a word. I poked her, but she was far away. Her eyes were green, like flowing water, like a precious stone, and she swore and spat when she was angry with me and, actually, I would have preferred to be alone, but when she slept on my knee and I gazed at those gossamer eyelashes, I thought she was the most perfect thing in the world. While she slept I took hold of her locket to see what was inside, but she knocked my hand away in her sleep. Once when they had disappeared I went to find them. I was always afraid of losing my way when I left the car, so I took a blue string to trail out behind me. One time I found them, and they were sitting on the bank of a lake and talking like two adults. I accidentally stepped on a branch that broke with a loud crack and she saw me when she turned. Then she looked back out across the lake and they carried on conversing as though I didn't exist. I stood still, as if there were a secret force field surrounding them that kept everything in the world away, including me. All this made me think that she was much older than she purported to be. I walked back to the car and after a while he returned with her asleep.

"Who's the older one of us?" I asked that evening, when she had woken again and was sitting cross-legged on the bonnet in the sun, spinning my globe to determine where we were going to go. Father smiled at me as if I were an idiot.

"You are, of course."

"I was thinking that there are small people."

"She's just really quick and impressive for her age. You were too."

"Was I?"

"You were, yes, you were totally outstanding."

*

The rearview mirror revealed rows of fir trees and a white sky so low that the treetops were snared in a cobweb of mist. Johnny was sleeping on my knee, and now, after driving all night, we had reached the morning, which advanced slowly as the roads disappeared behind us, with a scent of freshly opened flowers.

"Don't you think Blanche misses her?"

He avoided my eye in the mirror. His eyes were screwed in the harsh light. More screwed than normal, for Father's eyes were always narrow, as if he had a secret in them. He had. All people have secrets. But every time a secret is uncovered, new secrets rise up, and for that reason there is no point in prying.

"Blanche needs a holiday sometimes."

"So what about school? Shouldn't she be going to school either?"

"You two are far too brilliant for all that stuff."

In what way we were brilliant I never discovered, nothing beyond the assurance that we were. We were special, exalted, unique, delightful and superior to all of those whose orderly lives we drove past. I had learned it all on my own through the newspapers, about physics and world history and everything else, and sometimes I thought it was as Father said, that I knew more than all the others my age, that I knew everything. But sometimes it struck me how little I knew; I didn't even know where we came from or where we were going, or where people went when they disappeared. Long ago I had started accompanying him on his nocturnal drives in search of one more night, one more sunset, one more work of art, one more new acquaintance, something serendipitous that you didn't believe existed until it appeared out of nowhere. There were all-night museums in those days, and all-night libraries. We saw Nefertiti at a midnight exhibition, we browsed through ancient books in empty night-time reading rooms, and above all else we saw the world return with the light after being drenched in darkness. The whole time we were inside the shimmering bubble that was my father's mind.

I was woken by their voices. She was sitting in the front and on her knee was one of my birdcages, looking huge in her arms. A waxwing on a perch followed the car's movements as we swung round bends, the shiny little feather-body tilting slightly to the right and left. She and Father didn't appear to be talking about anything in particular. Just about things we drove past: horses, trees, poppies. I dozed off again and was woken by her hanging over the back of the seat wearing Father's sunglasses.

"Are you awake now, you sleepy roe deer?"

We stopped at a little guesthouse surrounded by a park

with pendulous, drooping fir trees. Spending several nights in proper beds was the best thing we did, like submerging into soft water and drowning in down and silk. We sank under the surface and disappeared from each other. We gave ourselves up to sleep, defenceless. When Father drew back the curtains and light flowed into the room, it might have been a second that had passed or many years. Johnny was still sleeping on my arm, the sun shining on her triangular face, but she didn't wake. Even when she was deeply asleep, her eyelids were slightly open, a chink where the eye-light shone clear. She didn't wake, despite Father clattering with his razors and opening the window with a crash. Some days she suffered from a strange fatigue, as if she were inhaling ether or some other anaesthetic, but I wasn't worried. I knew that for certain people sleep is a refuge, as it was for Mother when she turned away from me and was sucked into another dream. It is the only freedom we have; in sleep no person can reach you, no hands, no words, no laws.

There was a bright blue swimming pool at the guesthouse, a gigantic azure eye that lay gazing up at the sky. After breakfast I woke Johnny by shouting in her ear. She was a little grey in the face from sleep, but happy, animated and high-spirited, and when she discovered the pool she rushed over to it and leaped in, still in her cloak and dress, and swam around like a little dog. I had a new bathing costume; it was bright yellow and went transparent in water. I had found it hanging to dry on a motorbike at a filling station and I couldn't go past without taking it. I had given my old one to Johnny, but she didn't want it. I was good at stealing things – I knew how to avoid getting caught – but it was all ruined once it came into my possession, swept up in a whirlwind of things that didn't go together and remained meaningless out of context. I had tried to give Johnny many of my old clothes, but she only wanted her own outgrown, old-fashioned dresses and dungarees, which was why she looked like an adult in miniature and meant her clothes were stretched and tight. She must have grown at record speed that summer; I reckon it was the sun. There was so much of it all the time, as I recall. Perhaps she was also standing at one of those thresholds that exist at certain ages, when you are about to become a completely different person. "Bye-bye, stupid costume," she had shouted and dropped my old yellow bathing suit out of the open window as we drove through a grey industrial landscape. I turned and saw it flutter away in the wind, hit a lamppost and fall to the ground. "Why do you throw away everything that I give you, Johnny?" She stuck her nose in the air and glowered out of the window, but since we shared the back seat we couldn't escape one another and soon we would take up where we had left off. I would continue to give her new things which she would throw out of the window. It was just like Father and me; we had been doing the same things for so long, we couldn't remember anything different.

We practised lifesaving in the swimming pool with Johnny pretending to be dead, and when she did she was so heavy, I couldn't keep her head above water. I was seized with terror every time, even though I knew we were practising, and I had the sudden feeling that an immense hand was touching her from afar, wanting to take her away. When I had brought her up onto the side of the pool, she still pretended to be dead and that hand brushed against us once more, an ice-cold gesture out of nowhere.

"Stop it now, Johnny!" I shouted.

She opened her eyes. There was something indecipherable in those eyes, something in them I didn't understand. A penny for her thoughts, a dragonfly for everything there was inside her, a snow-white bird if she told me something I didn't already know. Her eyes were uncannily green, crystalline-clear irises, polished emeralds, and her pupils dilated and contracted when she looked at me, as if she was slowly adjusting her aim.

"I can't save you anymore now."

It was like peering down into an ocean, into an alien world, into eternity.

"Do you want to drown with me, then?" she whispered.

Father was playing tennis at the hotel and we were lying next to the court to dry off. We were the daughters who had just got to know one another and, much as I wished she had never turned up, I was scared of something happening to her. Her presence created a special kind of watchfulness, and made me think about things I hadn't thought of for a long time. The obvious: my mother. Naturally I wondered if she still thought about me. And then I spent a lot of time thinking about Blanche. I tried to ask Johnny, but she didn't want to talk about her. I had always thought children were chatty and expansive in a quite frightening way, but not Johnny; she was worse than Mona Lisa with her secrets. Now she was lying on her stomach on the grass, counting to herself. The clouds scudded past like huge carriages on high, a psychotic sky. She was counting everything she saw that day, like a little mathematician: trees, clouds, hours, words, insects.

"Who are you really, little bunny?"

She counted on her fingers in silence.

"Have you been to school?"

"That's five words."

"I know that you can count, but you can't have any secrets from me."

She made another calculation.

"Fourteen."

"I have told you I can read your thoughts, right?"

"Nine."

"No, ten, you clown . . . You do know that Father has a gun?"

She forgot to count.

"I go to school. This is my summer holiday."

That night I caught an adder. I used Father's tennis bag to keep it in as a temporary expedient. I thought it might be useful to have.

Time blurred. It was like the ocean we drove beside now and then, silver-grey motionless water with no beginning and no end. We each hung out of our own window and shouted at passers-by that they were arseholes and dickheads and hustlers. Johnny was fun to be with even though she was so young; she understood more than you'd think at first, sitting there in her cape with her little turned-up nose. And she learned fast. I taught her to swim properly and to wash her underclothes in the small can I used as a washing machine. I taught her how to smoke reed-cigarettes and cigars and normal cigarettes. I taught her how to catch and take care of insects and frogs and birds. I taught her to read and write, and when she had learned to write, she started to pen letters that she never showed to me. Whenever we came anywhere near a postbox, she would sneak a letter into it. Who was she writing to? Who did she have that she could write to? It didn't help to write letters, that much I knew. I thought I would teach her how to shoot, but I never had the chance to do that.

I dreamed we had stopped in a rest area. Next to my father and me the car boot gaped open like a giant maw. Inside was a roe deer, asleep. Where did it come from?

"It was just lying here," Father said loudly, and when the little Bambi heard his voice, it jumped up, clambered down to the ground and disappeared into the forest. In my dream we travelled on. That was what we did in reality too. Sometimes we did our washing in a launderette, and on those visits Johnny would sit glued to the machine, her eyes following the dress and cape and small slippers inside. It was our television. She loved proper television as well, on the rare occasions we came across such a thing in a bar or motel. She could stand for hours with her hands on the screen until I was afraid she would disappear inside it. And she could sit for hours and look at a creature dying in one of my glass jars. She liked watching at the precise instant it passed from life into death and grew totally still. It was as if in every moment and every place there was a little door to death, opening and closing right next to us. It gave the feeling of being able to make the whole world still.

One evening she said,

"Mother will be coming to fetch me soon."

"Who said so?"

"I did. But I'm going to miss you."

I felt sorry for her and sorry for myself, and so I said,

"Blanche will never come back."

I fell asleep with her head on my knee and the sound of a bird squawking incessantly in the back, a blackbird we had caught a few days earlier that was staring at us from its glass jar with its head at an angle, as if that might humour us. When I woke, Johnny had gone. At first I saw nothing because the bright sunrise was shining like a spotlight in my face. I heard the sound of the ocean, and when I looked down at my feet, I saw waves splashing into the car and over my shoes and my things. The doors were open and outside there was only ocean. My father sat absolutely still in the front. The sea around us was calm and steely smooth and a thin mist hung over the surface. I crawled into the front next to him. He turned and pointed to something moving away along the beach: a woman and a child hand in hand.

Their silhouettes grew smaller. It was Blanche and Johnny, and it was farewell. We said nothing, just sat there until it started to rain. Then Father waded ashore, walked to a telephone kiosk between the sand dunes and rang for a breakdown truck.

We were sitting in our car as usual, but now behind an enormous red recovery vehicle towing us to the nearest town. While the car was being repaired we went to the cinema. It was showing *Planet of the Apes*: apes in dresses, apes on horses, and finally an endless shoreline with a Statue of Liberty in ruins. We set off again to wash the car, which was covered in seaweed and sand, and for once I sat in the front with him. I had always assumed I would sit there when I was older. I loved it when the huge, brightly coloured brushes rolled in on top of us and water beat against the windows; it was like making a fresh start. We drove out into the sunlight in our gleaming car. I think my father had intended to drive out into the sea and just keep going while the car slowly filled up, but the salt water had mangled the engine. I had a vision of us there on the ocean floor, still strapped in and with our hair floating upwards. By some kind of miracle Johnny's letters must have reached Blanche, I thought. The adder in the tennis bag was dead; I had forgotten it. Next to it lay its skin, like a little overcoat it had shrugged off before going to sleep for a while. I used the skin as a bookmark.

At no time did my father and I ever speak about Johnny again, as though she had never been in our car, sitting bolt upright in her cream-coloured cloak. Not on the day she left and not a few days later when I found her locket on the floor between the seats. I held it out to him and for a second it was dangling from my hand in the pale light. For a second it would have been possible to see what she was hiding inside it, before he took it and flung it out of the window. Time dragged on in its fitful, runaway, indiscriminate manner. Sometimes I fancied I could see Johnny at the edge of the forest in her cape, standing beside a blood-red suitcase, but when I turned to look out of the back window, she had always disappeared. And when I think about it now, it was always – even before she came and went – as if we were driving to escape from something, as if someone was trailing us. But there was no-one who knew where we were or who we were, no-one who missed us or searched for us. My father imagined we were the centre of the universe, that the whole world actually revolved around us, that people spoke about us, that we made an impression when we rolled up in yet another little village. In his world, every-one knew who we were. But who were we? I didn't know and I never asked, for I didn't want to reveal my ignorance.

I always had a feeling that, out of all the stories, I had over-looked the crucial one, that I hadn't been attentive enough, and I didn't want to disappoint him. But we were always on our way somewhere, circling around cities on country lanes, along highways that no longer seemed to be used by anyone other than us. I often thought about the people who had built these roads at some point in the past, the men with their buckets of paint who made the lines that shone at night in the headlights. Where were they now? It was always there, and so intense, the absence of those who had created all this, the buildings and motels and filling stations and the grey roads.

One day her little face was in the newspaper. Her big round eyes stared up at me out of the printer's ink, her hair as iron-straight and glossy as ever.

"Hello little Johnny," I said, touching her, "little bunni-kins, where did you go?"

In the newspaper it was reported that her name was Holly, not Johnny, that she was eight years old but small for her age. She had been missing for almost four months from a coastal town, and the newspaper published a photo-graph of the house where she lived, in an isolated and exposed location by the sea. Everyone had assumed she was dead. People had gone missing there before, and a traveller had been held on remand all summer, but one day in autumn she had come wandering down the main road, clean, in one piece and unharmed. I looked at the date of the newspaper – it was already several months old. No-one had been able to make her talk about what had happened to her. All that was known was that someone had deposited her in the same place where she had vanished in a puff of smoke some months earlier. Her mother made a statement to the newspaper, her heavy features gaunt, like an animal's, an angry, starving fox. She was dressed in the same severe, old-fashioned clothes, but she didn't resemble Johnny (or Holly as she called herself now) in the least, glaring out from under a mass of frizzy, colourless hair, a grey, overblown dandelion compared to her daughter's lustrous tresses. "At first we thought God just wanted to borrow her for a while," she said, scowling out of the newspaper. Others in the area had been convinced that beings from another planet had kidnapped the child. Travellers, gods and extra-terrestrial aliens were the usual suspects when there was an unexplained disappearance. Blanche wasn't involved in any way. Blanche was simply some kind of tired spectre of my mother. Had these women ever existed? Later I saw Johnny's mother shouting out of a television set that the person who had kidnapped her daughter was a predator . . . a beast . . . a monster. I suppose that makes me a beast and a predator too. If anyone had asked me if we wanted to keep her, I'd say that I would have done anything within my power, would have given away my snake and bird collections, would have gone down on my knees and prayed to whoever was out there in the darkness. And if no-one had heard me, I would have taken her little hand and run into the forest.

You think things are going to last forever. You think you will remain the person you have always been, and perhaps that is so, even though the lay of the land around you changes and the river becomes fields of red flowers and they in turn become closed forests. I had my fifteenth birthday, my sixteenth and then my seventeenth. At night I dreamed my father was burning in the electric chair. One day I climbed out of the car – I hadn't intended to, beforehand, and I don't know why I did. My father was talking in a telephone box and I walked in among the trees and through a warm forest of tall pine trees and when it came to an end I carried on walking through a field of poppies and along a road until I came to a town. A bar was beckoning me, with neon lights and palm trees and cheap beer. I sat down in the bar and drank. I got drunk for the first time and it felt as though I had come home; the world turned upside down and radiated brightness, and for the first time there was a sunrise inside me. I had tried to find my mother, then Blanche and then Johnny, but in the abundance of sunshine none of them mattered. The bartender asked where I came from, and I told him the truth, that I came from all over the place.

"Tell me about all over the place."

It was the sort of thing you said without expecting an answer, an old song you sang without thinking about what the words meant anymore, if indeed you ever had. We played cards and, because I was too drunk to move on, I had to sleep at his place. He had a bed under a giant tree and a mosquito net had been hung up around the bed and the darkness was soft and gentle.

Now and then a car headlight sweeps over us from the road and illuminates everything in ghostly blue. When I lie here at night, holding a stranger who is sleeping faraway in a world without me, I can still feel the sway of the car inside me, rounding one bend and then another, just as the ground moves long after you have disembarked from a boat. The light from the setting sun transforms the rearview mirror into a flame. I see my father close his eyes and prepare to die.

EASTER

Every time I see a butterfly come teetering through the grass following its own law of gravity, I think that you can see us and that it's an eye into another world. Sometimes I dream I'm breaking into your heaven. Well, maybe not heaven. But you know what I mean. I know you do. Even when you were a child you said you wished that life would end, that it ought to have been over long ago. I've wondered what I should make of my life too, and many times I've felt like throwing it all away. Then I've changed direction and carried on. At your funeral I fancied I saw you standing outside the chapel in your black bomber jacket, watching us. I saw you quite clearly through the frost-covered windows. You had your hands in your pockets like you used to, and you were all hunched up, peering up warily under your cap. You stood there watching us for a while and then left. Now Easter is almost here again, our fifth Easter without you. I asked you once what death meant to you. That was what you were supposed to do, according to the psychiatrists. Talk about what happens next. Be specific. How they intend to do it. The consequences. "What do you think death will be like?" I asked. You said, "You fall asleep. You die. Somebody finds you." And that's what happened.

Today I was back in Skogås. I drove along the motorway through the forest and found the houses on the hill, where they have been since the 1960s. They have been repainted since I was last there, and now they are all white instead of brown. Below our old block with the narrow balconies was the steep slope I used to slither down in the snow to get to school at the bottom. We only lived there for one winter and spring in the 1980s and then we moved on. I rang Mum from there today and said I was standing outside our house, which was rising up towards the watery spring sky, the perspective slightly askew and the building leaning as if it was going to topple over.

"But it's incredibly dreary there, isn't it?" she said.

I thought it was nice – I always have – how the houses appear to be climbing up the cliff, how the sky is bigger there than in other places, how the solitary pine trees reach out to infinity. Some women were standing outside their doors smoking, their babies in their arms.

*

She had sat on the little balcony, watching the birds and longing to be away from there, while I had discovered the forests and the people living in the apartment blocks around us. You didn't exist yet, but our father would come by from time to time, and he used to stop for a few nights before he took off again. Where he was the rest of the time, I didn't know. I think he stayed with friends in town in those days. The centre in Skogås is a shopping mall now, since they pulled most of it down and roofed it over with glass just after we moved away, but the pet shop is still there by the newsagent's next to the station. As kids we would stand there all afternoon watching the birds and the tropical fish. We used to cycle to Drevviken lake, where the pine trees grew right down to the water's edge, and we floated on our backs in the black water. A boy at school was electrocuted in the power station one night and he stopped growing after that. For one second he lit up like a burning angel and then he dimmed. Miranda's father was in Beateberg prison, so close to us that I would cycle past every day and try to catch sight of him through the narrow, barred windows. And yet he was as unreachable as if he dwelled in another country. Our house was in Västra Skogås, on the hill, and the residential area was on the other side of the tracks. The rails formed the divide between two worlds, but the centre we shared. After school I went down to the tracks and arranged a line of stones in an attempt to make the train derail. I think even then I was testing my powers, wanting to know if I had power over life and death. The whole world bounced and shook when the train came hurtling out of nowhere, and for a moment you could imagine it sweeping you away with it, into something unknown, but a second later the landscape was still again.

Once, when I had to take the train myself, some old guy sat in front of me and played with himself the whole way into the city. It was almost summer by then and our apartment was already full of removal boxes. The sun filtered through the grey-streaked windows of the carriage. We were alone in it, apart from a group at the other end who were laughing loudly together, and I didn't dare stand up and walk away. He reminded me of someone – I couldn't think who – and it was as though I had frozen to the spot, bum in seat. It wasn't until Riddarfjärden opened up beside us like a mighty mirror that he rose to his feet, fastened his trousers and went to stand by the doors. I waited until he had gone and then I got off, jumped down onto the track, leaped onto the next platform and then across to the next. But, as though he had cloned himself multiple times, I kept seeing him the whole of that summer: resting like a languid crocodile on the side of the public pool at Forsgrénska Badet, his face half concealed under the water, sitting at the back of the bus on the way out to summer camp, standing right at the top of Västerbron bridge in sunglasses, waiting in the rain under an umbrella at the bottom of the Nationalmuseum steps.

The year after we moved away from Skogås, the commuter train finally did derail. We saw the photographs in the newspaper showing the train on its side among the trees, looking somewhat rejected and ashamed, as if it had tried to run away but been stopped by the green ash – by the gods, I was going to say. My mother folded the newspaper. She was done with all that, now that we lived directly under the sky in the city, at the level of the birds and the light. It had been a long spring, the spring of Chernobyl; the prime minister had been assassinated, Challenger had crashed into the ocean and my father was in the nuthouse. We visited him there – the place was called Ulleråker – and every time we went, we got lost among the numerous buildings. We never asked for directions and we never brought flowers. That spring I had the feeling that the whole world was going down the pan along with my father, who was sitting there like a fallen king in his threadbare hospital gown, staring into another galaxy. He used to say that there was a special order in hell and, at long last, he had been assigned his level. He said he had inherited Fröding's old bed. He spoke so fast it was difficult to keep up. But after he had been buffeted around for a few months in the tempests of the Second Circle, life carried on, he was resurrected, rather like trees are in spring, and he met your mother. They moved into an apartment on Kungsholmen, next to the filling station by Norr Mälarstrand, and there you were born.

I travelled through Skogås sometimes with Zacke when I was in high school. We used to go to the jacuzzi and the gym and the tanning place in Handen and the quickest route went past Skogås centre and the church, Mariakyrkan. People knew they had arrived when Beateberg appeared on the cliff above the motorway like a giant bird's nest, and I used to wonder whether Miranda's father was still inside. I could smell our old life, the raw odour coming out of the rock the houses rested on, the lonely, bumpy train journeys into the city, the spring days of gritted pavements, the single mothers who looked like matchstick figures from high above. There was no real centre in Handen; the buildings looked as though they had been tossed randomly around the station. It was chiefly the three-storey solarium where you could lie as if in a laboratory, enveloped in wonderful radiation. We lay there, floating, like nuclear babies. Sometimes you might hear someone having sex in the next cubicle, but I usually fell asleep in the blue sun. The exercise area was empty and bare. We lifted a few weights and from there we slid into the jacuzzi. Once I accidentally had an orgasm on one of those exercise machines in the gym, and then I stopped doing any training and I sat by one of the mirrors and watched Zacke work out instead. He was slightly chubby and had a hedgehog haircut and he died when he was twenty-four. I don't know what happened to him – we had lost contact much earlier – but even back then it was hard to imagine him having a proper life.

I had nicked him from my best friend, but she didn't know yet, so we would go to Handen for the day because we needed to get as far away from her as possible. He picked me up below Södra Latin high school and we drove around rather aimlessly in his borrowed car. Outside, the spring shone with an ominous white light. He didn't have a driving licence and never would, and I had no idea what to do with him now that I had him. It is one thing to take possession of someone, but love is quite another thing, something that takes an entire life to understand. We tanned, he trained, and we both went in the jacuzzi, and in the evening we drove on to the pool hall. Tom sometimes came with us, and if he did, I did nothing but wait for him to leave. Time didn't exist in the darkness of the pool hall and neither did we as we sailed between the green tables with a beer in one hand and a cue in the other. Zacke was phenomenal at pool, he had been in a competition, and he stood chalking his cue for so long that an entire life could be lived around him. And now you were in the world. When my father and his wife needed help, I walked around in the city centre after school with you in a pram. I kept waiting for you to wake so that I could lift you up. I had waited for someone like you for so long and now, at last, you were here – I must have looked like a young and happy teenage mum.

On the way home Zacke used to make a quick visit to a man living above the solarium in Handen, who supplied him with strips of pink pills that he washed down with Coca-Cola. I never found out what he did in return for the tablets – I waited in the car or hung over the balcony – but I know he would have done anything, no matter what. I believe he would have done anything for me as well, if I had asked him to, but I didn't know what I wanted. I wanted to have it all and I also wanted to throw it all away. I never took any tablets, a lesson I had learned from my father. It was just that we drew different conclusions from what we had learned, my father and I. He ate tablets like sugar cubes and he used to say that the pills had saved his life, them and the alcohol. When we were back in the car and Zacke had swallowed the small pink capsules, he leaned back and closed his eyes. I could see the little tablets slowly descend inside him, then he put his foot on the accelerator and, for a few seconds, our bodies were too heavy for the forward momentum; we were forced back into our seats and it felt as though the shadows of our former selves were left there outside the solarium forever.

Zacke told me he had bought sex from a girl on Malmskillnadsgatan. Tom had been lying on the back seat under a blanket, eavesdropping, and she, the girl, had sat on top of Zacke in the front. He was proud of that purchase; she had been sensationally attractive and from Poland and a little bit older than him, and Tom had been in a horny trance in the back. He had staggered out of the car afterwards as if out of a heaven. They went on to make several such trips and Tom chickened out each time, until finally he was forced to crawl out from under his blanket and clamber into the front. There he sat with his inert and useless willy in his hand, crying with shame, while Zacke laughed at him. It was Zacke's favourite story.

There were so many butterflies when I was a child, but by the time you were a child there were very few and now they are almost gone. When we visited the butterfly house in Haga park, you could wait indefinitely for a giant butterfly to land on you. You sat absolutely still on the floor with your hand outstretched while the other kids rushed hysterically back and forth between the tropical trees like little idiots. I didn't have the same patience as you did with butterflies, so I took out a book and sat and read to pass the time while you waited. It was *The Unbearable Lightness of Being*, and after many pages in Prague with Tereza and Tomáš and Sabina, a double butterfly landed on your hand. It was two butterflies attached to one another in some kind of elaborate act of love.

"Look!" you shouted, and everything seemed to stop with your smile.

The butterflies were almost as large as your head, and yet they appeared weightless in your little hand.

You loved all animals, even those strange insects disguised as small gods. For me, even then, you were quite unreal; you were five and then you were six and you started school and I still wondered where you had come from. Once I let you come to the university with me and you had to crouch down by my bag under the desk because my teacher wasn't fond of children.

"Is that your kid?" my desk-mate asked.

"My little sister."

"She looks like a tiny elf."

"I know."

After the lecture we took the bus to Gröna Lund. We went on the ride that swings you out over the water in a suspended seat, where you are fastened to the world by only a thin cable and, spinning around out there, it felt as though we could lose contact with the earth's gravity and disappear into the sky. Back on the ground, we felt slightly sick, but we had another go, and another, while rain fell on the city. Your swing was flying next to me like a mechanical bee and you looked at me with so much trust, it hurt. On the boat home you fell asleep on my knee.

There was a butterfly we called little Apollo, the little space-traveller, and you chased it along Hantverkargatan and into Kronobergsparken. It was actually called the Mnemosyne butterfly, the same as the goddess of memory. It was she who invented language and words as a protection against death. On the way home from nursery you ran out into the road to catch it; you had suddenly forgotten about the existence of cars, of the world. A lorry braked and came to a halt a metre away from you, and a woman climbed out of her car and yelled at us. You looked at her, slightly disoriented. It was the first sign. There would be many more.

Sometimes I babysat for you on Kungsholmen and I would sit in the bay window facing the water and study while you slept. You always had difficulty sleeping when you were small – I think it was because you were scared of falling into the darkness on your own – and when it was assumed you'd been asleep for ages in your room, there would suddenly be a streak of white light in a doorway, as if you were disappearing round a corner, a little ghost gone on a walkabout. I followed you to your bed, where you had formed your pyjama jacket into a basket filled with biscuits you had found in the kitchen, and when I looked into the room a while later you were still sitting cross-legged looking out into the room like a miniature Buddha.

"Can't you sleep?"

"I don't want to sleep. I want to stay here. With you."

"Shall I lie with you for a bit?"

We snuggled down and I fell asleep too, and when we woke your mother was there. She was the one you had been waiting for. It was already morning. The windows in the sitting room stood open to the water and the sun flooded in. My father was still asleep in one of the apartment's darker corners. He and your mother were about to split up, and later, after he had moved out, I would often feel like a stranger in your house.

At times during that final spring, you lived with me. You slept in one of the children's beds when they were with their father. You lay there curled up with your computer and your mobile phone, under a child's quilt, surrounded by cuddly toys. You used to get up some time in the afternoon and then we sat and talked in my kitchen until you went back out into the night. I knew that you were on your way, but I didn't know how to stop you. It was as if you had set something in motion long before, and what remained now was just a question of gravity.

"Are you coming back?" I asked, when you were standing in the hall in the evening, with an unlit cigarette in one hand and your tote bag in the other. *God hates bags*, it said on it.

"Yes . . ."

"When?"

"Soon."

"How soon?"

You smiled, and there was such light in you. I wonder where that light would have taken you if you had still been here.

"Don't you want to see the children? They've been asking for you."

"Not at the moment. I can't face it."

"OK."

"I'm going now."

I wanted to hold on to you for a second longer.

"Do you really think God hates bags?"

You smiled again. "Yes, most of all."

*

Later you wrote that you had wanted to stay for my daughter's sake, and I believe you. You travelled light – there was just you – and I often think to myself that you intended to slip out of the world without anyone noticing. Sometimes, when I wish you were back, I feel as though I am in one of those old jokes. A Swede, a Frenchman and a German are on a desert island and a genie grants them each a wish. The Frenchman and the German both wish to leave the island. And the Swede wishes for them to come back. Then I think it doesn't matter what I wish for; you're not going to come back anyway. All the same, I sometimes think about what would happen if you did, but it becomes increasingly difficult to imagine. The world you left behind is defined by your death: the flowers that have grown on your grave, the small insects that buzz from one flower to the next, everything that has happened without you. I had that last spring with you and it is such a blessing now, your final gift.

One night, Zacke and I slept at Tom's in Jordbro. We climbed up through a fire hatch and lay on the roof under the stars, dozing in the summer darkness. I heard them talking about me as I fell asleep, and their voices made me feel safe, as once upon a time my parents' voices had.

"But her breasts are way too small," Tom whispered. "Haven't you thought about that?"

"But fucking cute, though," Zacke whispered back.

"You can hardly see them with her top on. Not like the Pole. Remember her?"

"Yeah, yeah, shh," Zacke said.

"Shut up," I muttered, and they did.

We were woken an hour or two later by the first rays of sun.

"Turn the fucking light off," Zacke mumbled.

Hundreds of birds were dive-bombing us – there was bird dirt everywhere, on our blankets, in our hair – and we ran down into the apartment and went back to sleep in Tom's bed.

The other night I dreamed we were back together again, Zacke and I. We were standing by a pool table in complete darkness, as if we were hovering alone, outside time, and a small band was playing Bruce Springsteen. Zacke took my hand and pulled me onto the dance floor and we danced slowly. He had the wonderful scent of men's cologne, and we were no longer children, neither of us; he was the man he would never become.

"Don't forget me," he mumbled into my ear.

"Never," I said.

He held me at arm's length, but continued dancing.

"Don't you want to know how I died?"

"Yes."

"I was shot in the chest up near Mariakyrkan, you know, where we always used to drive past."

"Were you?"

I looked down at his chest, which appeared intact under his top, the same Black Sabbath top he often wore then. He pulled me towards him and held me tighter.

"No. It was just an ordinary overdose. Two hundred Rohypnol. But that would have made a better story for you."

I don't know why I am telling you all this about Skogås and about people who have died. I had actually meant to write about Fröding's sisters, who are buried next to him in the Old Cemetery in Uppsala and whose names didn't appear on the gravestone for many years. I had Fröding's lonely Eden on my mind and the seven young women who wrote to him under the name of Astrid, as if they were one young girl, full of hope. And Strindberg's sister Eleonora, as she was called in *Easter*, the woman who destroyed her sculptures every year. I was thinking back to her death alone in the asylum in 1904, just after Strindberg had written *The Ghost Sonata* and divorced from Harriet Bosse.

SARA STRIDSBERG, born in 1972, is a writer, playwright and former member of the Swedish Academy. Her first novel, *Happy Sally*, was published in 2004, and her breakthrough came two years later with the publication of her second novel, *The Faculty of Dreams*, the English translation of which was longlisted for the Booker International Prize in 2019. Her novels have been translated into 25 languages, and she has been shortlisted for the prestigious August Prize three times, including in 2012 for her collection of plays, *Medealand and Other Plays*. She lives in Stockholm.

DEBORAH BRAGAN-TURNER is a translator of Swedish literature, and a former bookseller and academic librarian. She studied Scandinavian Languages at University College, London, and her translations include works by Per Olov Enquist and Sara Stridsberg.